Praise for *Bone over Ivory*

"With wit, sophistication, and a welcome lack of pretention, Jack Kohl takes us on a Cook's tour of how literature and music can intersect. His love of the classics—be they literary or musical—shows through on every page, and his ways of associating what he plays with what he reads is quite remarkable. Perhaps no musician since Ives himself has written so movingly of why Transcendentalism still matters. Performing musicians as well as students of American literature will adore this pithy offering on the altar of art."

—Philip F. Gura, author of
American Transcendentalism: A History

"If Ralph Waldo Emerson had been trained as a classical musician instead of a theologian, he might have written much as Jack Kohl does. Kohl runs marathons, falls in love, walks on beaches, writes novels, but in these intimate essays his universal impulses get expressed through metaphors shaped by the visceral feel of fingers touching keys and ears piecing together melodies. When he compares running through the woods at night to piano playing because the roots of trees feel like black keys to the feet, you realize that we musicians process the world in a different modality."

—Kyle Gann, author of *Charles Ives's Concord: Essays after a Sonata*

"Henry David Thoreau, who Jack Kohl references many times in *Bone over Ivory,* asked "What is there in music that it should so stir our deeps?" The same question can be asked about good writing about music. Kohl's seven essays form a tone poem supporting two main themes: music and the musician (in this case the author himself), art and the artist. And though, like in any good tone poem, the parts may be brilliant on their own, together, as a whole, they shine. *Bone over Ivory* tickles like music itself. Read it and listen. And then go play your favorite piece of music."

—Jeffrey S. Cramer, editor of *The Portable Thoreau*

"The pianist and novelist Jack Kohl has given us a provocative and thoughtful book of essays, finely written, and following unexpected paths."

—David Dubal, Author of *The Essential Canon of Classical Music*

"Jack Kohl writes about music and performance with a dry wit—a rare thing these days—embroidering his wry, pianistic observations on life and even love, with Dickensian syntax and a sprightly turn of phrase, that is rather endearing in today's bankrupt age of Twitteresque banality."

—Brendan G. Carroll, Author of *The Last Prodigy: A Biography of Erich Wolfgang Korngold*

"It's wonderful to read Jack Kohl's beautifully crafted prose. I'm particularly biased, of course, to 'A Transcendentalist's Love Story,' that uses Boston's iconic Parker House as a setting!"

—Susan Wilson, House Historian, Omni Parker House

"Author-pianist Jack Kohl brings together his mastery of classical piano repertoire and his love of fine prose to create a rare marriage of two art forms. Reading him is an exciting intellectual experience."

—Michael Johnson, Author of *Portraitures and Caricatures: Conductors, Pianists, Composers*

"Jack Kohl writes with a rare sensitivity, elegance, and intellect, revealing a deep understanding of the piano and its literature, and an appreciation of the curious hold this instrument has over those of us who play it."

—Frances Wilson, pianist and writer;
"The Cross-Eyed Pianist"

BONE OVER IVORY

Essays from a Standing Pianist

JACK KOHL

THE PAUKTAUG PRESS

Pauktaug, New York

Published by:
The Pauktaug Press
Pauktaug, New York

ISBN: 978-0-578-47354-3

Cover illustration: Freiman Stoltzfus
www.freimanstoltzfus.com

Interior design: Gary A. Rosenberg
www.thebookcouple.com

Printed in the United States of America

Contents

The Liszt Sonata in B Minor: At the Temple Door

Piano practice is like having a dog. If one has lived long enough with such an unnecessary but at the same time critical circumstance, one wonders how others live without the seeming obligation. Thus even when concert work figuratively dies for me—when I have no cause to go to the piano for considerable stretches of time—my hours and days are still ruled by its unnecessary-necessary compulsion; just as my life continues to be ruled by a dog who has recently passed away. I rise before I need to rise, for fear that he who is now only a ghost may need to go for his walk. And when I do not practice, my mind is still hounded by the Liszt Sonata in B Minor. I think about it, and it still influences my daily conduct even when I have no obligation to the quality of its sonic or physical recreation. It is always the ghost dog, the Man's Best Friend, of my midnight walks in my village. But in the case of the Sonata, it is I who is led by a mystic tether. One's walks are then guided by the unseen, as one is pulled away from the obvious and straight courses of sidewalks and streets—sent overland and over-yard to any shrub or tree that beckons. The Liszt Sonata pulls me that way. It is the piece I practice even when I do not practice, when I do not listen to its recordings, when I do not consult its text, when I do not hear it in red velvet recital halls. Only after all these activities are in the past does the best part of music study take effect. The Liszt Sonata in B Minor influences my conduct beyond my responsibilities as a pianist—and acts as a reference point for my ethical and practical choices. For it is the principal tuitional grist I carry about in my conscience, the principal written record from another mind that I consult outside of my own stake in the great pool of Reason.

I discovered Liszt's Sonata in B Minor in my early teens, when an itinerant uncle stored his records in my family's home. From out of his crates of LPs I pulled Agustin Anievas' recording of the work. I was made a pure apostle after one hearing. By age twenty I first performed the Sonata. And nearly thirty years later I made a study of all the commercial recordings of the piece I could find. But how does a piece of musical abstraction influence my conduct and beliefs?

So much has been written about the Liszt Sonata in B Minor that I will only pause at the doors of the temple to make my case as to its personal influence. I cite only the two complementary descending scales delivered in the opening bars: *G-F-Eb-D-C-Bb-Ab* (bars 2–3); and *G-F#-Eb-D-C#-Bb-A* (bars 5–6). Even one with rudimentary piano skill can test out these two scales for himself. We need not give the theoretical names usually applied to the scales above, nor the precise registers or rhythms of their rendering in the score. The notes alone will do. The Liszt Sonata is the sole work in which I find the subtle yet vast potential of modality to be nothing less than a suggestive miracle.

Note the static letter names shared by the two scales. But the astounding and piquant chromatic differences between the pair steal across the ear like the founding of a Faith! The two scales stand in analogy to translations. Of late in my runs in the woods I have thought that a translation is like a bushwhacked path that lies near and parallel to a blazed and groomed trail. The blazed path is the original; the parallel bushwhack trail is the translation. For the latter has the same course and distance as the former, but it forces leaps and jumps and differences upon a run of the same aim. One trail is in the language of man; the other is in the tongue of deer hooves. Or perhaps the bushwhack trail, with all its roughness and peculiar meanings, is the original. The opening scales of the Liszt Sonata in B Minor are like such parallel trails; they are translations of one another. Yet they are both utterances of an abstraction. They are as translations wherein neither one nor the other is necessarily the original. The comparison of this pair in succession is the *only* passage in music that makes me cock my head like the RCA Victrola dog—and really mean it. But whose is the master's voice I recognize?

There is vast debate in the historical literature as to whether the Liszt Sonata in B Minor follows a program. But if even just these opening scales fuel a thrall in the private mind that neither the one *nor* the other is the original, could the listener or player, then, via the most careful attention, identify with the impersonal scales in a proprietary narrative spiritual sense? Is Liszt's greatest achievement as a programmatic composer, as a tone poet, his mastery over a musical second-person language? Does he invoke sublime generosity? Does he tell *your* mind's intellectual program over *his* motivic foundation? And thus in making it uncertain which of the paired scales is the gold standard and which is the paper, does one start to feel the stirrings of a reassurance, that the body is not a mere original for a hoped-for spiritual complement? By making the original of something in music uncertain—the same in letter-names, but different in exquisitely slight and magically chromatic ways—perhaps I have more faith that a mystic counterpart is also sure to follow or precede or coexist with my fleshy self? My body shares the same space with an enharmonic ghost? My modal soul shares the same space with a carbon shape? When I am outside of the temple doors again at the Sonata's end, and hear the final utterance of these scales, I feel no fear of the grave.

There is something of the better-or-worse optometrist's question in these first two scales. One is still looking at the same chart of letters as both scales goes by in the Sonata's opening, but

Liszt is figuratively flipping the lenses on the same letters, on the same row in the chart—inviting one to look at a group of finite symbols through shifting chromatic prescriptions. "Sit still," Liszt seems to sayeth. "Yet I will make things grow within, though they seem to shift without whilst keeping their identities."

There are intuitional means by which one may grapple with mortality. But the Liszt Sonata in B Minor is the only source of guidance from tuitional means that has reconciled me soundly to an end—to dissolution as necessary, in manner beautiful, part of the process of gaining comprehensive and ultimate humility.

Charles Ives's "Kŏn'kôrd" Sonata: The Vestibule of the Temple

I would not write an analysis of Charles Ives's *Sonata No. 2, "Concord, Mass., 1840–1860"*; I would write only a praise. This work has been as a dorsal fin in my existence since I was in my mid-teens, serving midway between the pectoral influences of Ralph Waldo Emerson on one side (through his Journals and published essays), and Franz Liszt on the other (principally through his Sonata in B Minor). Emerson and Liszt have always seemed men ripe for a study of parallel lives in crab canon: Emerson of Concord, man who metamorphosed from minister to performance artist; Liszt of Weimar, retired performance artist bound for a near-priestly twilight.

The "Concord" has always appeared to me formed by a Liszt Sonata in B Minor that escaped from passage on a mystic *Mayflower,* hid then between the serrations of tribal arrowheads, next amidst the lines of Puritan sermons, at last reemerging through Ives as his Second Piano Sonata when the old Calvinist headstones in the churchyard turned like a piano's pins from the torque of Transcendentalist tuning hammers. It is no coincidence, I believe, that the "Concord" Sonata of Ives starts on a B-natural, on the same pitch class as the Liszt Sonata's conclusion. Everything that follows in the Ives work has always seemed to me as an atomic subdivision of that final note of the Liszt Sonata.

How did I first learn of the piece? The Easter Bunny thought I had aged out of candy and left me a hidden copy of Howard Boatwright's edition of *Essays Before A Sonata and Other Writings by Charles Ives* on Easter Morning of 1985 or 1986. The Easter Bunny is wise. He knew me better than I knew myself. Ives wrote the essays "primarily as a preface or reason for" his Second Piano Sonata. Opposite the first page of each essay for the Sonata's four movements (an essay for "Emerson," "Hawthorne," "The Alcotts," and "Thoreau"), Ives gives the first page of the respective movement from the score itself. The moment that I first looked in silence upon the "Emerson" movement's opening five systems is distinct in my memory.

Ives's engraved note heads appeared to be independent of the staff lines underneath them. Somehow the score writing seemed to imply epigrammatic meaning without the context of staff lines. He appeared to record some kind of Journal-like impressions without heed to his notebook's ruled pages. That first impression from thirty years ago was similar to one I had of late. While rehearsing recently on the afternoon before a hastily prepared musical theater concert with Broadway actors, I was handed a printout for the song "Vanilla Ice Cream" from the musical "She Loves Me." Perhaps because the printer's ink cartridge was running low, or perhaps because the original scan of the music was faulty, the copy showed note heads that were distinct, though of a jaundiced color. But the staff lines were nearly invisible. It was remarkable to me how much the absence of the staff lines made the note heads useless to me as a sight reader. There was a rush to find another copy of the music. But for the first page of Ives's "Concord" one feels that there is a deep and artful implication from the seeming separation of the note heads from the sublimated staff lines. The stars at night are like such Ivesian note heads. Is it by some kind of Faith that we feel there must be spiritual staff lines between, around, the sidereal musical notation, inspiring our will to form constellations? And yet the actual lines are there if one looks twice with sober eyes at the first page of the "Emerson" movement. Ives's wild utterance is a heterodoxy brought into control by a Puritan focus. Transcendentalism only works in the shadow of the Meeting house; one cannot coast too far. But the harmonic verticality on that first page seems a sign that Ives will only enter as far as "the vestibule of the temple" on the grand staff.

His harmony almost seems a complement or foil to ubiquity: like soap bubbles that might conjoin yet not appear yoked (and not augment the size of the new sphere); like Siamese Twins with one body and one identity; as a game of Twister wherein all players could somehow end comfortably on one spot; or as if an entire flock of gulls could alight on one flagpole, yet not one bird crowded to the equator of the topping sphere; or as a snowball that admits of packing but does not admit of the snowball effect. In other words, what is the reverse of ubiquity for multiple objects? Rather than one thing everywhere at once (ubiquity); it is everything (or many things) at one place at one time.

Mitt-like width of chord spans are called for in "Emerson"—as if wider and wider parts of the body might be called upon to realize the vertical sonorities—as if ultimately the width of contact would be so great one would need be prostrate on the keyboard; and then one would need get up and live for themselves instead of the music. It is music that makes one stand up from the bench in health. It is as an object or article the use of which is to compel one to repudiate it in favor of one's own actions. But the act of repudiation is not an act of rejection. This music makes a noble sacrifice of itself for the listener's mind. It weans one like an aggressive mother bear its aging cub. The hands are so often splayed in very wide non-tonal contexts that the fingers assume the arrangement of one engaged in a handstand—as if one might look away from the score and the instrument and perceive the world upside down, as with the refreshed fascination as when one bends over to look through one's legs.

The width of the chords in "Emerson" is such

that they compel one to look at systems above and below the one is playing at the moment. Ives compels non-linear comparison of his own material in this way, and one is reminded of the unanticipated comparisons a reader can make when using any text, when, with fingers between the pages or just before a page turn or in the midst of a draft, intense sunlight reveals in retrograde the text that is printed on the reverse side of an oncoming page or a preceding page.

All this points to Ives's success in translating the miraculous effect of Emerson's latent prose mechanics. Emerson credits the best books with triggering thought, and he does not mean thought in relation to a book's subject or style—no, something in certain texts (something deep in their mechanics) triggers one's completely independent thinking of a reading—completely independent of a book's content, style, *and* even the latent mechanics that trigger the thought. Emerson's own books have that latent mechanics—as if while making demands for themselves they also trigger some part of the mind that is as a cerebral appendix to the conscious act of reading the book of another.

The "Emerson" Movement is programmatic

insofar that it suggests the mental mechanical action of the man Matthew Arnold called the greatest prose writer of the nineteenth-century—a writer who, if one counts the spaces, the periods, between his dense and intentionally incongruous phrases—has asked his reader an equal number of times to think as much if not more than the author. Most people, when saying prose writing is musical, mean to suggest an ineffable quality of poetic ringing or rhythm to the language. But Ives in his "Emerson" movement captures a deeper musical suggestiveness from Emerson's working habits as a writer of Journal entries—a mechanics that invoke an equal share of the horizontal and the vertical—and those mechanics somehow survive in latent evidence in the essays. To wit: Emerson's filling notebooks from front to back and back to front, writing of pages up and down rather than from side to side; intentionally stacking incongruous subject matter atop one another. Emerson calls upon the implied strength hidden in a palimpsest. Ives mentions in his own essays Carlyle's remark on Emerson's lack of coherence paragraph to paragraph. But the lack of coherence is intentional, and the tacit transitions are left to the reader—*and* the listener. Emerson's lack of coherence is not incoherence (the latter word suggesting cognitive instability), but a conscious effort to remove articulations of transition. The reader, the witness, is forced to live in that gap and to realize transitional surface himself.

If in lieder *word painting* endeavors to express concrete meanings of a word by the direction—up or down—of musical notes, then Ives for Emerson *transition paints*. He endeavors to catch the metaphor leaps that are left to the reader by Emerson when the reader is confronted by unsequential sentences on a related topic. Ives recalls the moment of an erudite squirrel leaping, in mystic but somehow unbending portamento, from tree to tree in Mr. Emerson's orchard. Ives renders the leaps of a "La Campenella" into a dance betwixt one's own neurons.

I spend a lot of time trying to disabuse students of the misuse of the word *song* for non-song pieces. But in the "Emerson" Movement of the "Concord," perhaps the usage is correct in an unsuspected way. For Ives undertakes a prosody for the latent mechanics of Emerson's prose. Emerson's latent mechanics—the mystic text buried in the infinite density of his periods and semicolons—are not detected by "reading between the lines." That phrase merely suggests the ulterior purpose of the visible text. Emerson's and Ives's latent mechanics ask that the reader, the player, the listener, synthesize mediating purposes that are aggressively omitted.

Granted, the foundations of profound abstract borrowings from spoken and sung language had long been laid in piano literature. The frenetic machinegun alternation of the hands in the first page of Ives's "Emerson" may even announce a philosophical leap of purpose over the nineteenth- and early twentieth-century piano performance practice of left-hand-before-right-hand execution.

But Ives's intentions are much more ambitious than those of the pianist-composers who borrowed from and steeped themselves in the bel canto tradition. Ives does not seem to imagine the rhythms of Emerson the lecturer, of Emerson the performer. Again, Ives's aim appears to be the translation of Emerson's latent mechanics into music.

Emerson himself, in his remarkable entry (from *Journal Y,* 1845–1846) under the heading of *Croisements,* writes: "The seashore, and the taste of two metals in contact, and our enlarged powers in the presence or rather at the approach & at the departure of a friend, and the mixture of lie in truth, and the experience of poetic creativeness which is not found in staying at home, nor yet in travelling, but in transitions from one to the other, which must therefore be adroitly managed to present as much transitional surface as possible. 'A ride near the sea, a sail near the shore;' said the ancient."

Ives's "Emerson" movement codifies and achieves this aim. By means of what might be styled a Total Chromaticism, Ives paints as if from a palette, fires as if from a quiver, of all leading tones. The listener must learn to exult in Ives's painting in "as much transitional surface as possible." I remember as a child that I was disappointed that one could not land on Jupiter, could not set foot on a gas giant—for from afar it looks like a glorious and inviting solid. But it cannot be mapped. Ives's score, in imitation of the latent prose mechanics of Emerson, is a snapshot of an evolving surface of Jovial ether. The "Emerson" movement, though the first movement in the Sonata, is in fact a development section in disguise yet in plain sight. Its repositioning is a mild and superficial disguise, yet as effective as Clark Kent's glasses. It is a development in which the founding elements are constantly resetting, as if it is a record of incipits, of all beginnings, of all first bars. It is like a language of all prepositions—nay, *pre*-positions.

Mass. is a common abbreviation for *Massachusetts*. But I suspect Mr. Ives, in his Sonata's title, is rendering a civil religious pun. For he has given us not just a piece about Concord (kŏng'kərd), Mass., but a work to be regarded as the Mass of concord (kŏn'kôrd)—best heard from the vestibule of the temple.

A Transcendentalist's
Love Story: Sonata Form

I would like to share a love story—framed by two solitary moments (separated by fourteen years, two months, three days, and sixteen hours) before the same telephone in the same hotel room in Boston, Massachusetts. But, to begin with, let me go back to the first meeting I had with the young woman.

I met her in a museum, in Ralph Waldo Emerson's house, in Concord, Massachusetts, on May 22, 2003, a few minutes after 10:30 AM—just three days before the bicentennial of Mr. Emerson's birth, and three days after my own thirty-third birthday. But I hope no one will think that I believe I can parallel Mr. Emerson on any greater terms than that small coincidence.

I had been to the house a number of times before. I lived by this man's words and knew that his house was no more a shrine than that it was proof that such words as his could be written in common rooms. But on this trip, when I saw the lovely tour guide—I see her now in memory in a long black skirt and black cardigan sweater—I encountered a kind of feminine beauty that I did not expect to find while paying homage to idealism and to my stoic compass.

I knew the tour well, so in desperation I forced myself to invent an esoteric question about the lore of Concord. In view of an open closet, in which Mr. Emerson's dressing gown was displayed, I asked, "Where had been the asylum, the poor house, in relation to these grounds?" It was an absurd question, but she tried to answer, and it helped her to remember me later. Two rooms on in the tour she asked me where I was from. I am from Long Island's north shore. At the top of the second floor's stairs the guide asked me, below a portrait of Charles Sumner, if I recalled the name of the man who had caned him on May 22, 1856. I was too flattered to be able to recall the name of Preston Brooks while under pressure. I then marveled at her voice and her fingertips as she pointed to a bust of Mr. Emerson by Daniel Chester French.

"That is the face that I shave," Mr. Emerson is

said to have observed upon assessing the skill of the likeness.

I parted from the guide in the main hallway of the house, but not before answering to the remainder of my trip's itinerary—that I wished to visit the Old Manse on Monument Street and to pay my respects to Walden Pond—and noted her answers when I asked how it was that Concordians pronounced *Sophia* (*So-fye-a*) and the family name *Keyes* (*Kize*).

I left the house and the young woman, and I endured what I decided had to be a pardonable regret, for I could not think of how it could be rectified. I lived two hundred miles away. Still, I lingered for a few moments in Mr. Emerson's garden, and thought of the young woman as she had stood below and pointed up to the old fire buckets on the tour. I considered the cliché that a mermaid would pause under sources of water—perhaps with a rose pinned behind one ear and a daisy behind the other—and though I had not even shaken her hand in goodbye, I imagined that some trace of her iridescence had remained upon my fingertips. For as I had listened to and looked upon this young woman, I fancied the frame of the house had been infused by her viscerality and that it had become as the wood of the world's most ancient and pedigreed violins: on some mystic-microbial level still living, still infused with some vital and Greek-pure libidinous will even after centuries. I imagined this infusion spreading beyond the bounds of the house and spreading through all matter in the village, reaching unto the Musketaquid River just beyond the Mill Dam.

I drove down through Connecticut and returned home by crossing the Long Island Sound by ferry. It did not occur to me, then, that from Concord's Egg Rock, the river systems make their way at last to the sea, and that salt water connects to all salt water quite directly, that her iridescence had means to follow. I did remember that in many a Sonata-Form movement a quiet and brief Andante section often precedes a massive and principal Allegro.

My parents are of Pennsylvania origin, but, again, I was born to Long Island. That left me a solitary, native, figurative orphan of Paumanauk. I knew that Queequeg of Ahab's *Pequod* entered his first American whaling port in Long Island's Sag Harbor. And I have often fancied that I am one of the descendants of the children outside of Jay Gatsby's wake room in East Egg. Reports Nick Carraway with the appearance of Gatsby's father: "I took him into the drawing-room, where his son lay, and left him there. Some little boys had come up on the steps and were looking into the hall; when I told them who had arrived, they went reluctantly away." Fitzgerald's Mr. Gatsby has long been high on my list of the great Transcendentalists, both fictional and actual, a careful list that includes Ralph Waldo Emerson, Captain Ahab, Henry David Thoreau, and perhaps, too, Master Yoda of Dagobah.

As a very young student of Gatsby's Transcendentalism, I knew that the book carried, for someone like myself, a greater and more severe Venereal caution than any biological horror I was warned about in health class. For I was too hell-bent on my piano studies in youth to get into common trouble. I think of Horowitz's remark: "I trust musicians more than anybody. They practice too much to do harm." In my teens and twenties and early thirties I practiced too much to suffer common harm, but I practiced too much to prevent the accretion of a greater and later kind of mythic risk.

I knew from my Fitzgerald study that "Gatsby turned out all right in the end. . . ." But I had not yet studied the subtle nature of how that end was earned, or learned for myself what would make Mr. Gatsby, for me, the highest of American Transcendental Priests.

By the time of my 2003 trip to Concord, the fierce routines of my youthful practicing were behind me, and untested and ostensibly held virtues were about to have performance trials upon life's platform. For I knew Mr. Gatsby's ultimate Transcendentalism for myself as does a pianist who has mastered a piece only in the practice room. First performances often reveal a compromise of nearly fifty percent of control. I had had my romantic scrapes, but even as a thirty-three-year-old man I held a full and intact heart, and only a half-tested gospel in my head.

May 2003 yielded to June 2003, and I still thought of the young woman in Concord. I who loved Emerson so much, he who said, "Our first journeys discover to us the indifference of places," and loved so much *what* it was he said, lost my indifference to the place where he said it—I who come from a village of such beauty that if I were to lose indifference for a place it should only be my own. But I still thought of the chiseled fingertips pointing to the fire buckets, and in my walks by the Long Island Sound I fancied more and more that touching the water left traces of mermaid's skin upon my hands, a subtle material like lost contact lenses from a thousand delicate dolls. When I had stood upon the shores of my native village, New England had always pressed down upon my imagination and my shoreline like a branding iron. I am surprised that its intensity has not steamed off the Sound. The north shore harbors are proof of the pattern of the iron, the mark of the brand. I live on the edge of Cow Harbor.

With all this in my mind, I went to my desk on a June night and looked up the address of Mr. Emerson's house. Not since, perhaps, Walt Whitman had any native Long Islander written to that Cambridge Turnpike address with such hope and interest. In the letter I described the tour I recall above, and near its end I remarked: "One travels through life and has these little meetings, and they go by in silence and compound into little yet grand, poignant yet powerful regrets. Again, I hope you do not think this silly." On the envelope I could only address the tour guide by description, for I had no name.

I mailed the letter on June 3. I heard nothing for more than a month, and I did not really expect to hear anything at all. On July 10, however, I had a reply by email. As I look now at the boxed records of our correspondence, from even just the month following that reply, I see the history of a romantic quickening without precedent in my life. The Andante preamble before a looming Sonata-Allegro form was subject to an *accelerando* as by the most welcome case of stage-nerves and excitement I have ever known.

I was fascinated by the caution of our telephone conversations when compared with the romantic character of our writing correspondence. I remember that the young woman asked me with care when we first spoke if I had the intention of practically emulating a Thoreau, of hoping to test life at its fundamental level by living in a cabin. I replied with levity: no, that I had already known too much of the woodshed from all my years of practicing. But even in those calls there was an ardent acceleration, and we suggested that our conversations recalled the earnestness of children with cups and strings in place of phones between neighboring windows.

Soon after our correspondence began, we agreed to meet in Boston, on August 5. At her suggestion, I made a reservation at one of Boston's venerable old hotels, the Omni Parker House, and we made our appointment to unite in its lobby at 3:00 PM, after she rang my room to announce her arrival. Romance apes the satisfaction of creative activity; thus I cannot express the electric idleness I enjoyed while waiting for my journey.

I made my preparations as the Andante *accelerando* continued. At last I travelled by an early morning train from Penn Station, New York to Boston, along the same rail path of George Gershwin's ride during which he conceived the plan for "Rhapsody in Blue."

Wrote Gershwin: "It was on the train, with its steely rhythms, its rattle-ty bang. . . . And there I suddenly heard, even saw on paper—the complete construction of the *Rhapsody,* from beginning to end. . . . By the time I reached Boston I had a definite plot of the piece, as distinguished from its actual substance."

When I myself reached Boston, I took a cab from South Station yet followed my own definite plot to the hotel on School Street. "Here on business?" I was asked during check-in, yet I do not recall my reply. I was sent to Room #1151, which even then had the numerical significance to me as that of a bar number in a score.

I was so in awe of the mounting importance of the occasion that I unpacked my suitcase and used the room's chest of drawers. I had never thought to do that in a hotel before; nor had I ever seen anyone else ever do so. I took a walk in the nearby neighborhood, and I remember the cuckoo calls of the crossing signals. And I recall being afraid that I might see the subject of my appointment before the specified time. I had lunch, and I returned to the room to prepare.

The small room then was as a greenroom before a recital. I showered, and I dressed with great care. I had new clothes for the meeting. I had put aside Thoreau's advice: "If you have any enterprise before you, try it in your old clothes." I had a new polo shirt, as white as the top C on a piano in a showroom. But when I added my new black trousers, my torso looked like the base of the white-key D between the blackness of D-flat and E-flat.

This brings me to where I began this tale, to the first time I was before that room's phone, waiting for it to ring. My heart beat as if I were running 200-meter repeats on a track, though I did no more than pace. And yet I wished to hold that moment, to live in the eve of event, to hold back the most anticipated of things.

3:00 PM came, and the phone on the little table next to the bed's headboard rang: "Mr. Kohl, your party is here," said a man's voice from the front desk. I took a last pause and checked myself in the mirror, and then I went to the elevator. I had never found elevators of particular significance before in my life. Yet I must attempt to say how much occurred on that ride. Lobby buttons and descending elevator rides have now a remarkable suggestiveness to me.

I muttered a few hellos to fellow passengers as I made the descent, but permit me to share the truth. I must now steer away from applying mere mermaid clichés to the young woman who waited for me, for they are inadequate, and I should apply the focus of figurative language to the subject for whom I can confirm all facts: myself. I have said that I had made it to that point of life, my thirty-third year, with my heart completely intact. Thus I can say that I was then as the supposed Chicxulub

Impactor of sixty-six million years ago, as the speculative asteroid that arrived to mark the end of the reign of non-avian dinosaurs—as the stone of fate that landed to mark the Cretaceous-Paleogene boundary in Earth's history. I had been safe on earlier visits to Massachusetts before my last trip to Concord, for only an empty house was there, an orbit I could escape.

That elevator ride was as that Chicxulub Asteroid's final descent. I shook with magic. I burned and sparked with friction as I fell deeper into the air of that lobby. I was affected by the once-in-a-lifetime resistant material of an atmosphere. But the volume of my heart as fatal asteroid was such that no atmosphere could burn it up before it could make its strike.

The elevator came to rest at *L;* the Chicxulub Impactor made its landing. The doors opened. I stepped into the busy lobby and its Yucatán waves of people, its lighting to me like that of a Merchant-Ivory Edwardian amber. We had joked days before that we would find each other in the darkest and most private corner of the lobby. There were no such spots. Nor did I need to look for one, for the young woman was the first thing I saw as I stepped forward. On the opposite side of the lobby—on a settee parallel to the front entrance and to School Street, but perpendicular to the row of elevators—she sat below a painting of the hotel itself. Her face was already turned to mine.

Her hair was as brilliant as a Ginger Rogers publicity still, as blonde as the rich and grained and warped light in the bell of a French Horn under stage lights. There was a rectangular, rose quartz, Malaysia Jade pendant on her neck, and her crossed legs emerged from an olive green shirt dress and were tipped by black shoes, and on one visible tiny joint, there was a single glistening toe ring. It had been a very hot day, and her skin showed a sheen. But her skin showed more than this. Her makeup had sparkles, had glitter in it. The dying mermaid's scales were shining now, reflecting the sparks of the Chicxulub impact. There was even sunburn in one spot of her tan—from the mermaid too long on the surface, as the mild burn as from the ash of impact, just to the right of her sternum. All the impact fire was wiping out the last of the mermaids—yielding a new species for Venus worship as yet untold.

She stood to meet me. I said her name with caution, almost uncertain if this could be the same young woman. She said mine, and then embraced me and then my palms, and placed a book in my hands: *Literary Trail of Greater Boston*. But then she kissed me. Unlike Jay Gatsby, however, with the kiss I did not "wed unutterable visions to her perishable breath," but wedded she who ostensibly breathed, too, the Platonic visions and herself romped with the mind of God. The great abstractions could take shape from her, as if her kiss would be to taste bardic epigrams at their human source, the transfusion from her kiss far more ambitious than any resurrection she could grant to the wood of an ancient house. I had not put her on a pedestal; I had thought to stare up to one with her, to raise one with the help of her arms, limbs carved in living sexual beauty.

Yet with that kiss I sought to balance unpardonably a spherical mass as that of Jupiter's onto a golf tee. Her makeup, with its glitter, impressed itself into my white shirt. And with my kiss, *my* asteroid's landing, my incarnation, I wiped out the dinosaurs.

But though I have taken pains above to draw some critical distinctions between myself and Mr. Fitzgerald's scenes, I was very much surprised, like Nick Carraway on his first night in Gatsby's mansion—when he entered "a high Gothic library, paneled with carved English oak"—to find a chance bystander on hand; this bystander, too, defined for me by some hint of supernatural placement and role of judgment. In other words I also had a witness like Nick's man in "owl-eyed" spectacles.

As my incarnating kiss concluded with a staccato click, a voice from one of the wing chairs, perpendicular to the critical settee, blurted out with humor: "Wish I could stay to see the end of this!" We three all laughed, yet I was certain the man meant something much more than a mildly prurient joke. I have never forgotten him.

The Andante preceding the formal Sonata-Allegro was over. I was in the thrall of a perceived form now, in the grip of an irresistible Sonata Exposition. From that August 5 through the morning of August 8, the evolving Mermaid, a new species of Woman, shared Boston with me.

On the night before my departure, I recall that we visited the hotel's mezzanine. In the hallway there is a large mirror, said to have been in the hotel's rooms in which Charles Dickens stayed during an 1867–1868 reading tour. We tried to photograph ourselves in the mirror. I have the photograph before me now. We are hidden behind a flare in the picture, covered perhaps by the orbs celebrated in ghost hunter photos? Or is the camera's flash merely hiding our faces? I know for certain it is the latter, for it is the more supernaturally telling of the possible explanations.

And later, sitting atop the tightly made bed of Room #1151, tight like a drumhead—sitting atop tucked and curved legs, as if upon vestigial seductive flukes—the young woman invoked a parallel between our own new love and the romance of Emerson and his first wife, Ellen Tucker Emerson. I replied that I resisted the comparison because I did not wish to lose my love so soon. Ellen Tucker Emerson died of tuberculosis not long after their marriage. Emerson later had the courage to open her coffin and confront the metamorphosis of her remains. This gesture is thought to be so critical to Emerson's development that the incident serves as the opening to Robert D. Richardson's great biography of the master.

But we addressed our happy tears with the room's box of tissue. With laughter she dubbed the box the *Official Tissue of the High-Strung*

Transcendentalists. She inscribed a bicentennial Emerson exhibition book to me: "On the 200th anniversary of Emerson's birth, starts the new journey together of Emersonian discoveries and Transcendental triumphs."

Now permit me to take one up to the moment I faced the phone in Room #1151 a second time.

After a romance of thirteen years, conducted over distance *and* proximity, gift book inscriptions began to be written in pencil, and the young woman began to pull away in earnest. I fought unremittingly, even fanatically, against this—for a year and at a distance, to the point it was self-defining. But, curiously, I could win neither success nor valediction from her. And somehow the strength given to the figurative fingers of mind by my piano study permitted me to endure an interminable cliffhanger.

I leave the story of the intervening years of our romance to her. I do not omit so much as I do not presume to guess; this is the story of an individual consciousness, at last. Should she share the story with you, I contend that everything she will tell you of me is true—but her reproaches will not be harsh enough and her praises will not be high enough.

"I am not a Transcendentalist," she said. I had come to know this already. But that didn't mean I did not love this woman for herself. Yet that also did not mean that she did not tire of a man who *is* a Transcendentalist. I was true through it all, despite our troubles, for I loved the actual woman, as much as my illusion. I fought so hard because I fought as for two things, for twice the lover's usual stake. And thus, with an unanswered proposal in the air, and with the positive side of her ambivalence fueling my nature, I expressed one last suitor's plan by telephone.

On the Sunday afternoon before Columbus Day, 2017 at 3:00 PM, would she ask for me at the front desk of the Omni Parker House in Boston once more? If she did not appear, I would cease my pursuit. She acknowledged these terms—set for a week away—told me she loved me, and we ended the conversation. I did not notice at the moment I made the plan that I set the appointment for 3:00 PM instead of the 4:00 PM appointment time I had made in 2003. I still think about that small detail.

So much of our romance had been defined by my phrase, "We are only just getting started," that

I prepared that week to march as if only to the repeat sign at the end of the Sonata-Form Exposition. On Monday, October 2, I met a friend from my elementary school days on the edge of the harbor of my native Long Island Village, and he warned me not to make the journey to Boston. But he said later that because he knew me well he also knew that I would go. A pianist's practicing teaches a morality of form so intense that it insists one even endure the consequences of unearned error and pain. I was taught to observe the repeat signs in a sonata. A pianist does not listen to a piece; he studies it, thus even fourteen years can seem as a moment to him. And a pianist studies a holy literature but is never guaranteed a congregation by his conservatory; he must be ruthless and solitary to find a pulpit. So, yes, even after fourteen years, I was just getting started.

I took Gershwin's train again, and I took a taxi once more to the Omni Parker House Hotel. I checked in at the front desk for Room #1151. That part of the plan, that I had reserved the same room, I had kept to myself. The woman at the front desk did not ask me if I was there on business. The room was not yet ready, so I bided my time at the nearest bookshop and bought a gift, a volume I thought in keeping with the young woman's profession.

I ate lunch at the same address as I had on my first day in 2003, but the restaurant itself had changed. I returned to the hotel, and the room was ready. It was with a rare sense of wonder that I beheld the interior of Room #1151 again. Everything that I experienced in the preceding fourteen years had occurred since I had been in that room. Some objects were different or had been moved about. But the bed was the same, and it still sported the two symbolic New England pineapple carvings on the top ends of the headboard. And looking toward the bed, next to its right side, on the side away from the window, still stood the night stand and the telephone.

I hung my clothes in the closet this time, and they dangled there like Mr. Emerson's dressing gown in Concord. With some hours to spare, I went for a run, and I recall that my return route was blocked by a Columbus Day parade. I went back to Room #1151, and began my preparations for three o'clock. I showered and shaved and dressed with a greater sense of ritual than a groom in any culture. I chose to wear all black.

Perhaps so that the sparkles would not show as clearly if they came a second time? I looked like a walking fallboard from a Steinway concert grand.

I prepared the room as three o'clock came closer still, as I came closer to the expected meeting with the Exposition's repeat sign. I sat and consulted some of the very Journal pages I have used to write much of the above. More than once that day I felt an uncontrollable urge to cry, and more than once in the final stretch of preparation, I indulged myself. After 2:30 I tried to watch television for a bit. I took a momentary solace in Alec Guinness' voice as Obi-Wan Kenobi during the climactic dogfight over the Death Star. At ten to the hour I stood up and began to pace. The small bouts of tears had taken the place of the nausea that precedes performance for some pianists, so I felt ready.

At 2:55 my cellphone rang (I had not even owned one in 2003), and I risked taking the New York City call. It was from my piano professor from my undergraduate years. That it was he—once a guide to me in the unseen shapes of musical form—who had called in these very last moments before the end of this mystic Sonata Exposition, was a seeming symbol not lost on me. I did not tell him where I was, but I hinted I had to observe a strict 3:00 o'clock appointment. We said a pleasant and innocuous goodbye after a few minutes of speaking. I remembered for a moment that I had studied Beethoven's Sonata Op. 7 with him.

I resumed my pacing and then stopped and stared at the phone at 3:00 PM. Even the two parts of the receiver suggested to me the two vertical dots of a score's repeat sign. I stood perfectly still at the fork of a great musical roadmap, ready for a lesson from the Cosmos to proceed by command to *Da Capo*.

I muttered to myself, "Do the right thing." And I waited.

The phone did not ring. I waited until 3:30. The phone still did not ring. I thought of how I had recently heard a recording of Beethoven's Op. 7 by Andor Földes. He had not taken the Exposition repeat; that had jolted me. I went down to the lobby, and I looked at the settee below the painting of the hotel. No one I knew was there, nor was my owl-eyed man. I waited there until nearly 5:00 PM. I felt the deeply disconcerting sense a pianist suffers as during the onset of a memory lapse. But this was not a memory lapse; the piece had lapsed. I was astonished at the new details I noticed in the lobby as I waited in a state of raw but formless sound and vision.

I knew then I was no longer in a Sonata-Form. I left the lobby and wandered about the foreign city. I went to the McDonald's nearest the Old Corner Bookstore, the old location of Ticknor and Fields. As I ate, I noted to myself that the children repeatedly visiting the soda machine were of ethnicities that would have been as exotic to earlier Boston Brahmins as if those children had been baby Queequegs from Kokovoko. But these children with their Cokes and Sprites spoke clear and native Yankee.

I wandered back to the hotel's lobby. I thought perhaps to see a familiar face, panting with lateness. Yet I saw no one, not even my owl-eyed man. It was Sunday night, and I looked into the dark windows of the hotel's closed bar, *The Last Hurrah*.

Before returning to the room for the night, I visited the Dickens mirror again. In the glass I saw only the face I shave; I saw only what Luke Skywalker saw during Yoda's test for him in the Dark Side cave on Dagobah: one's own face.

In Room #1151—the number hardly seeming like a bar number to me then—I passed one of the most peculiar nights of my life. I lay on the bed like a melancholy chump and thought of Emerson looking into the coffin of his wife: he passing that test, enduring metamorphosis by accepting the disintegration of material most dear. I fancied the room then as the coffin of the beloved, but the body was nowhere to be seen. The woman had slipped the net. The dead was living out of sight. What, then, was the exact nature of my own test?

When I woke at times into that formless night, I turned musical phrases in my mind, as one does when sitting at a piano at the end of a working day, too tired to practice, pivoting infinitely between the suggestive leaps of an aged Tin Pan Alley song, a song, say, like Irving Berlin's "The Melody Lingers On"—or lingering repeatedly over the mawkish changes between a IV-chord melting into a disguised half-diminished seventh chord built over the second degree.

I rose early the next morning. But just as I finished with the shower, I was compelled to rush to the front of the room, for there was a knock. Yet it was only the bill which had been left under the door. I looked at it; the total looked high. However, after even the greatest debts are paid honestly, they never seem quite as expensive to me in retrospect.

I decided to abandon the gift book. Room #1151 now has a library of two volumes: a Gideon Bible, and a book about Early American Furniture. The elevator ride was gentle, and I left the hotel. My train was not for many hours, so I wandered about the city, dragging my little suitcase along on its wheels. I stopped before the front of Macy's, for there one can see a small sign marking the site of Emerson's birth. I looked into the store's windows as I had looked into the Dickens mirror at the hotel. No Mr. Emerson manifested himself as a transparent blue figure like that of a *Star Wars* Force Ghost. But it was not hard for me to imagine that a Master Yoda might appear to speak in his place, for Mr. Emerson was said to have little faith in personal immortality.

"Why," asked Master Yoda in his retrograde syntax, "walking in his house were you? And why, Master Waldo asks, no one alive living there now?"

I smiled as the Jedi Master's vision vanished, yet he still offered no answer as to what had been the nature of my test on this journey. I made my way to Boston Common. As I entered its precincts it began to rain! But the rain began to settle a bit of the Chicxulub Impactor's dust. Yet I like to think that the dust, the sparks, the glitter, had never been foul. The rain started to dispel, too, the remembered amber light of the Merchant-Ivory soundstage in favor of the soaked gray setting that often drenches a sad-sack in an ending that starts many a modern romantic comedy.

Even now, well into a new year, I have nightly dreams of fire buckets and an elusive figure who will not speak to me. When I wake, I always reproach my subconscious: "Tell me what I don't already know." But it is very rare that one can place the apostrophe after the *S* in the word *Transcendentalists*. So let me report what it was that I already started to think on that Columbus Day morning last autumn.

As I reached the crossing from the Common to the Public Garden, I did my best to match my mysterious test to a plot from one of my actual or fictional Transcendentalist hero stories. And I compared them all, at last, to one from the figure I must rank, still, at the very top: Mr. Jay Gatsby. For they all, all my heroes, had had their Daisies—even Master Yoda, I suspect (though *Star Wars* lore as yet gives no clue to the youth of the supreme Jedi).

Emerson's Daisy (his first wife) died, was removed for him, and then he became the man one recognizes; Thoreau's Daisy (his sweetheart, Ellen Sewall) rejected his proposal, and then he became the man one recognizes; Ahab's Daisy (the whale) kills him, and he remains the incomplete Transcendentalist, a figure incapable of escaping his object of singular focus. But Gatsby, I argue, is able to let go of a Daisy himself, for he "turned out all right at the end" indeed:

No telephone message arrived, but the butler went without his sleep and waited for it until four o'clock—until long after there was anyone to give it to if it came. I have an idea that Gatsby himself didn't believe it would come, and perhaps he no longer cared. If that was true he must have felt he had lost the old warm world, paid a high price for living too long with a single dream. He must have looked up at an unfamiliar sky through frightening leaves and shivered as he found what a grotesque thing a rose is and how raw the sunlight was upon the scarcely created grass. A new world, material without being real, where poor ghosts, breathing dreams like air, drifted fortuitously about. . . .

This moment may sound harsh at first, but not when considered in the light of a Transcendental triumph. Gatsby is no ghost—the Daisy is a daisy again. The Daisy is a daisy is a rose. He is at last awake. He has reached the level called for by Thoreau in *Walden,* that one anticipate Nature herself. It is likely that the passage above was written in a room over a garage in Great Neck, on Long Island. Merry poor houses, asylums, cabins, cometh everywhere.

I reached the bridge that crosses the pond of the Swan Boats in the Public Garden. Perchance the test was that I should conclude that the woman in my story had given me the gift as that of Ellen Sewall to Thoreau? Perhaps. But I still felt there was a need to solve the greater test, to give form to the formlessness that presided after the Sonata-Form had disintegrated.

The rain came down very hard at this point, and I ran to shelter under the awning of the nearest building next to the Public Garden. But as I stood there, wet and feeling foolish, thinking of concert pianists as no more than Franz Liszt cover bands, something made me think of a form I had dismissed from my first semester of undergraduate music history, dismissed because the ancient form rarely if ever served my instrument's more glorious Romantic utterances. I refer to the *Cancrizan,* the Crab Canon.

The simplest way I might express the formal shape of a Crab Canon:

GFEDCBA

ABCDEFG

Both of the above lines are meant to represent two musical lines sounding together, moving parallel, and in the same direction, both moving forward in time, yet the top line recounts the information of the bottom line in reverse order.

As the dust of my singular Chicxulub Impact continued to settle, I realized I had been living in fear of the assertion that we are living in a Cosmos where things are continually moving farther and farther apart—that impacts will be increasingly rare and one day impossible. But we are living falsely in fear of an ever-expanding Universe. We are as the forward moving yet retrograde voice in the Crab Canon—reconciling opposites and thereby all circumstances, reckoning all things that bless or befall, accepting the inevitability of forward motion whilst at the same time hinting at the reconstruction of the point of origin. All outcomes are indifferent so long as there is consciousness. We live in Crab Canon complement to the unfolding Universe. The Cosmos expands at present in its presumed cycle; we contract and restore it by power of metaphor, linking the ostensibly unlike and distanced and separated, marching away yet toward our founding singularities forevermore. We ourselves become a greater gravity than that governing Creation.

Under the awning some iridescent pigeons had taken shelter. "Do not the birds sustain the dinosaur line even now?" I muttered. I was relieved my owl-eyed man was nowhere in sight. His second and final appearance in Fitzgerald is for Mr. Gatsby's burial.

And then, perhaps because the boy Gershwin first fell in love with music on hearing the "Melody in F" of Anton Rubinstein from a player piano, I whispered a phrase of Rubinstein's from his twilight: "I have lived, loved, and played." Then I replied with some words of my own: "The greatest pieces are those which are not yet written."

Wrong Notes:
Principle over Sequence

As a pianist, I have spent a lifetime reading interviews given by other pianists. I would like to know, above all, what it is precisely that others think about when they play. People often ask *me* that question. I do not know if I have ever answered fully before giving what follows.

I believe that all great piano pieces and all works of art at last, for the thinking person, recede back into their component parts from nature. They are at their best for us when they reach this stage. And thus great works of music and art only become truly valuable when they start to bore us—when they disintegrate figuratively in our mind's hands like a clipping of overused and sweat-soaked newsprint.

When I perform an ostensible masterwork I feel that the piece passes by, but I do not. And yet as it passes I know that all its parts are always still ahead—as if any work is a closed loop, like an oval track on which one runs: one is always headed for the ground they have passed. The sensation I describe may be akin to one walking in the midst of a grounded and tame flock of pigeons. The pigeons surround one as one walks and feeds them in a park, yet they maintain a static circumference of distance and safety around oneself at the center. As one walks forward some of the front birds keep their distance by moving forward, some in the front by taking a position behind the walker. Some in the rear make up the ground by staying behind yet continuing to follow, some by moving up to the front. But always the circle is consistent in size. And after a time a walker feels that one does not move though one walks. A sense of universal starting point is felt though one is moving in an ostensible sequence.

A pianist is in the midst of *all* of the notes all of the time—in part because he has rehearsed the piece, already knows what is ahead and behind at all times. Could this be in part why a wrong note can continue to preoccupy a pianist even when he does not know why? Because he does not realize the degree to which his latently healthy non-sequential mind is inviting him to hear the work out of order even in performance, to recognize the illusory quality of all sequence in life? Does the superficial pianist respect too much the score, the superficial and ostensible sequence, respect too much the figurative map of the stars as they appear from Earth as fixed constellations? I think, yes.

I have thought for years about the remark of one my teachers, about his fixation with a wrong note early in a recital, because it would putatively befoul the recording of the event. But I submit he should have welcomed the preoccupation as a reinforcement for non-sequential suspicions. Perhaps the nature of practicing, of repeating, of rehearsing, fosters this suspicion in some pianists, and in any kind of worker who incessantly confronts cycles and repetitions.

A piano work's text provides a narrow path for the ostensible interpreter: rarely as wide as a narrow hallway; rarely even of the width of a well-worn singletrack woods trail. It is by custom as dictatorial as the course for a toy slot car. I suspect external factors projected by witnesses, listeners, cause the illusion of greater breadth of choice and personality from performers. How different, really, are the renderings of the greatest virtuoso from that of the simplest amateur if one really knows the material of the finite constellation of a score?

But an observant pianist is freed, in practicing, from perceiving a work only in sequence. Behold how many listeners have pined for such a freedom that they have been seduced at times by any rumor that secret messages can be revealed on LPs that are played backward. Even the manual technique employed to play a record backward is part of a universal suspicion that there may be freedom from sequence.

Having a series of successful sequential experiences which reinforce one's Identity can sometimes blind one to the supremacy of ultimate Principle. One becomes protective of any chain of good experiences; one becomes vain of them; one starts to become cautious so that they are preserved—as much in one's own hoarding mind as in the imagined storehouse of others. I recall a violinist with whom I played frequently in graduate school. He and I experimented with the idea of intentionally inserting discreet errors from time to time in a recital so as to prevent any accruing note-perfect performance from growing too unwieldy in the mind. But, at last, the wrong notes a performer leaves are only of value if he has done his best to avoid them. And if after striking genuine clinkers he realizes they are as the guideposts to a non-sequential perception of the world, then there is some hope for him.

But first a pianist must realize that the text is not the sacred thing in his performance; nor is his rendering. There comes a moment in any deeply-read person's life when texts no longer seem as representations; they recede into objects again. A reading text is no more significant at last before one's eyes than the space it occupies in the surrounding spherical range of vision at any given moment. The printed text ultimately has no more or less significance than, say, the light switch on a wall, or a tree seen out a window, or a leg of a piano, or any opaque object within the visible spherical range of the reader. Thus one can say all mankind is equally well-read. And due to an underlying sameness of all objects one can also say that an equality of reading history also applies regardless of disparity in length of life at death. Everyone has the same amount of reading. But how many have undertaken the same amount of synthesis? But a wrong note honestly earned, or any ostensibly deleterious experience in life, can start to point the way to the illusory aspect of all sequence, to the notion that Principle trumps Sequence always.

In performances that I have thought were going well in an early stage in a traditional sense, I began like a man reveling in the heap of sand that still resides in the top part of an hourglass, and marveling at the starting grains that fall in the first seconds of any flow, cherishing the sequence, hoarding what lies ahead. But then I was granted the masked joy of a wrong note. Then it is, for the thinking man, that the hourglass becomes as one held in outer space, outside of gravity, outside of sequence. The grains float and lose their ruthless power. The wrong note discovered honestly is the best note. It is the skeleton key to all. Our misfortunes, our ostensibly deleterious Experiences, never trump Principle. I submit that when one realizes this, there is no sequence, and one can never come to harm.

A weak man is devastated when something happens to him because it has happened to *him*. He may as an observer believe, in part, in Principle—hence another man's tragedy and *another*

man's wrong notes do not overturn his observer's
stability—but a weak man with only partial faith in
Principle over Sequence allows his *senses* to over-
whelm him when he is the subject of misfortune.
He misplaces identity in his senses. Identity is in
Principle. That way all Experience becomes Illusion—only grist and puzzle piece in the exercise
of metaphor perception. If one subscribes to the
notion that ultimate principles are common to
all, what difference if misfortune happens to *me?*
I do not grieve when another grieves—for I see
his experience as a symbol almost immediately,
almost immediately as a generalization. Yet we are
all conduits to the same few Principles of the light
and the good. Thus why should I grieve if *I* am
direct witness and subject to a misfortune? Being
a direct witness, a direct subject of misfortune or
any experience, is an irrelevant circumstance. If I
think with sober intelligence, my own experience
should also seem as immediate grist for symbol, as
well. The amount of time anyone requires to grieve
is in direct relation to his ability to convert *any*
experience into emblem. If one sees themselves as
an emblem even in the present then *nothing* can go
wrong for him. Again, if we all did not believe in

the supremacy of Principle over all else to some degree, another man's—even a stranger's—misfortune or tragedy would devastate us. I can walk a mile in another man's shoes yet find that the ground below is *still* the same. But a man who believes completely in Principle over Experience and Sequence is not devastated by his own misfortune or tragedy—not at all.

If one conquers the illusion that direct experience is any more harmful than secondary experience, then also a left-to-right faith in sequence is soon to fall happily, as well. If my principles are sound on, say, June 2 because no misfortune has come to me since June 1, my principles should be sound on June 3 as well even when I am a witness to calamity on June 2. Progressive perception of *personal* time and history says very little. But, again, we aim to play all the right notes; but welcome the skeleton key placed in hand by the clinker struck amidst noble aims. Knowing that any experience will or can be rendered into metaphor and ground down to its relation to Principle in an instant, a strong man going through turmoil will hesitate to confess it, for his confession of distress will soon be a lie to him. To a strong individual nearly all experience is instantly dated. Thus the emotional distance, invulnerability, of strong persons. Because of all this faith, I can say with sincerity that in almost *all* public and private conversation I am hesitant to use certain phrases—to wit: *That I don't feel happy; that I don't feel that it is a good day; that I feel I've had better days* and the like. And I do not mean that I conceal my real feelings, more painful feelings. Even if I experience such things, knowing them to be phenomenal, transitory, compels me to believe that I cannot use these common phrases because they will be soon false. I do not use them because they would conceal the imminently permanent truth. I say again that the degree of a man's insight can be recognized by the speed with which he recognizes any event—as soon as it has passed—for an emblem.

Disabuse ourselves of sequence even further! If everything we experience becomes an irrevocable part of the *past* as soon as it is past, which means just in an instant, why need say "that time heals all wounds"—as if that time need be significant in duration? By coursing forward constantly and superficially in time, we are offered health by the instant for everything, for everything becomes past, and thus an emblem, in a moment. Our nominally forward movement is always a blessing; we render everything at a constant rate into grist—mentally digitizing All without need of the cumbersome and fragile actual equipment of technology. All Experience passes over the shoulder as we move ostensibly forward—and even one's own body starts to pass over one's shoulder as it ages—even to a degree while in the best of health, and that is when an immortal mortal of invulnerability begins to be born. Even at death it is then as if one's own interpretative engine simply concedes one's person into an emblem. If we do not hold fast to the notion that Sequence is *always* trumped by Principles, we then slight the sound philosophy and happiness of those to whom incessant disasters have been presented, but who preserve the good cheer of the most sheltered man.

We may live in a Cosmos where no extinct species *ever* recreates itself—such is the tyranny of web and sequence—but this should not cause the individual to believe too much in that web and sequence as one's teaching master. If it imparts a lesson, it is only that each individual has a singular chance and a unique means by which to testify to an ultimate suspicion and faith that Sequence is illusory to thinking. One can stand at the moment of Creation even at time's end. Our birthdays are always ahead. We move forward constantly along an illusory Sequential line. That line runs down the center of an alchemical horseshoe of Mind; we face out from the open end. Into one prong of the shoe enters Experience; it leaves as Principle out the other end. We use the common phrase, "I put it behind me." Should it not be "I put it ahead of me"? Principle always lies ahead of us, and it futurizes all past things. We are always on an eve.

A sense of the overpowering supremacy of Principle and a suspicion about the fallacy of Sequence makes me feel that memories *are not* at last cumulative. They do not load into the mind like an ever-increasing set of figurative common Russian Nesting Dolls; memories are as figurative Nesting Dolls that are free from concentricity; they contain each other, but are of the same size. With figurative Nesting Dolls of the *same* size, all are present, but their mass and layering *do not* increase with their number. I think such an image is a key to good cheer in the strong man's mind: all Experience, all tuitions come in but are as naught—be they behind or ahead. They are all of the same size, and always trumping these finite-sized dolls in the mind is Principle—rendering moot any deleterious outcomes; rendering impermanent any accidental cheerful affirmations. So we move forward—must move forward—as collectors who at the same time do not take on weight though we are always taking on cargo. But there is no limit in the hold.

Indulgence in backward and forward time travel fables, and, I think, the tendency to fear ghosts, are all parts of an inability to live properly within the obligation of Sequence and yet to suspect and know its illusion. Most popular-culture time-related fables seek to avoid deleterious consequences and choices. I submit that the real underlying and benign suspicion of *Principles over Sequence* is that in a highly qualified and subtle sense there are no deleterious consequences to avoid. I even feel a weakness in myself when I indulge my interest in books of *Then and Now* photography. For their starting points, their *Thens,* have no real claim to *preceding*! I marvel instead after children's books in which the endpaper illustrations are the same at both ends of a volume.

When I say that I am happy to hear for the

Faithful that their Gospels may be true, but that I am indifferent if they are not, I mean this by *indifference:* I am indifferent to narrative reinforcement of Principle. If I woke up and found myself the only man alive at the height of the Cretaceous, alone as a man during the reign of dinosaurs, my feeling is that the demands of the Ten Commandments would still be true though they had yet to be spoken, and though I had yet to hear them. I cannot use narrative outcomes as evidence of Principle. Principle must survive negative evidence; Principle must precede positive evidence. Principle is a part of *no* Sequence. A man has more than the power of time travel if he believes in Principle. Principle spins the clock in all directions and also stops it. Principle does better than this; it obviates the clock. The weakest utterance a man can make is "If only!"

On Founding a Running Club: From the Journal of the Unanswered Question

For two years I was president of a member group of the Road Runners Club of America. I enjoyed my service, but I did not seek a second term. As my own interests changed, it became difficult to officiate over a club founded principally on a sport dedicated to finishing one's task as quickly as possible. I grew tired during certain workouts of being told that if I could talk, I was not working hard enough. I wished to run as I used to walk before I was a runner, going over the woods, beaches, and odd places of my native north shore of Long Island, near New York City. I had already run my Boston Marathon, and was now content to look north across the Sound for other reasons.

If I were to carry on with company on my new runs, I wished to find those content to run as a hiker won't, and with the willingness to stop as a runner will not. I wanted to go about slowly and look about carefully, and to hunt for arrowheads and fossils, but wanted to go where a runner can—which is everywhere. Wear running clothes and be in the act of running, and one can trespass almost anywhere, and one is already in the act of flight if chased. I wanted also to confine myself to a range, and realized I was blessed by the boundaries of an island. But with time I found that range unnecessarily large, and recognized boundaries principally set by Hempstead Harbor in the west, Mt. Sinai Harbor in the east, Route 25A on the south, and the shoreline of Long Island Sound at the top.

I could with ease contract this area much more, for some of my greatest adventures in running have come during loops on a track and even during the solitary confinement on a treadmill. But it has been unnecessary to pare down my range to that extent. Going over home ground repeatedly rewards the dedicated student. This is perhaps reinforced by the tendencies conditioned in me from my vocational piano studies, for imaginative repetition is everything in that pursuit. As pianist Marian McPartland paraphrased Bill Evans: "Practicing one tune for twenty-four hours is better than practicing twenty-four tunes in an hour." It is a good thing to practice such discipline everywhere in these times, for not since forty years ago, in the hallways of my elementary school, have I seen anyone use a pencil until it is ground down to the eraser. Today we never use things up. I cannot bear unfilled notebooks. And I note in myself the tendency, as well, that if I own two copies of the same edition of a book, I do not feel I have read the book unless I complete the reading in one volume. The same part of my spirit winces when I listen to so many of my compatriots boast of their travelling. *I* must remind *them* of place names when they share their own photographs. They ignore the wild in the near. There are now coyotes in Central Park.

Only one member of my old club followed me into the woods. After eight years of meetings, we remain a two-member organization with neither membership gain (though we have endeavored to recruit) nor attrition. Our club is known as *The Unanswered Question Free Running Compact. The Unanswered Question* part of the club's title references an orchestral piece of the same name by Charles Ives, and honors Mr. Ives's role as a trailblazer in music and philosophy. *Free Running* has also been part of our title since our founding in November 2011, and it was invoked without reference to or knowledge of the book and unrelated discipline conceived by Sébastien Foucan. We refer commonly to our group with the name shortened to *The Unanswered Question.*

The other member of the club, and its Co-President, is Mr. Peter Klann. In the woods, Peter Klann is *Mr. Klann* to me, and I am *Mr. Kohl* to him; the woods have taught us a mutual respect that leads to formality rather than away from it. Mr. Klann is a man who has worked for many years in the wholesale and retail vinyl record industry. The arm of a record player moves inward, following very fine groves, despite the centrifugal force of the turntable. This constant example of balanced forces, in part, may account for Mr. Klann's strength as a running companion. He is calm and steady in the midst of crowded oaks or straphangers. He is also able to assess the quality of a vinyl pressing without playing it. This may account for his observational powers amidst vast collections of autumn leaves. As well, I have noted to him, that though English is his only language, many of the principal people in his life—mother, father, fiancé—have been non-native English speakers, and would this not give him an advantage in detecting meaning over style? Over hundreds of hours on trails and shoreline I have learned slowly of his solid Catholicism. He is driven at times to wash the front steps of Our Lady of Pompeii Church on Carmine Street in Manhattan. After listening to me for the same amount of time, Mr. Klann has suggested I speak more in an Old Testament strain. Perhaps at our best, in certain rare moments on the trail, together we make for the faith of one whole Bible?

If pressed, I would identify myself as a Transcendentalist, that shadowy means of prayer defined, for me, by a comprehensive heterodoxy tempered by an unremitting conscience. Yet on our longer adventures, when the irreligious miles of return trips are often endured, we have merely passed much time pitting famous actresses on opposing Venus pedestals. For some time Jessica Alba reigned. But the game lost meaning after the invocation of Julie Newmar. For a time we reinvigorated the comparisons by announcing the contestants in voices that parodied Schoenbergian *Sprechstimme*, but that was short-lived.

One now has an appraisal of *The Unanswered Question*'s membership. Our meeting times? At the hours most conducive to traditional, to other kinds, of work, or in conditions most inclement to recreation. Time and weather can render any census false, so we pay in subtle ways for that advantage. The locations? Anywhere in the range given earlier. But none of the locations are so remote that one cannot leave the woods in some direction and ask for directions. Yet finding others is rarely a reassurance. We once encountered a man who volunteered guidance that contained no details, and in another instance Mr. Klann asked a postman if he knew the best way for us to regain beach access: "I only know the mailboxes," the letter carrier confessed.

Yet go to the woods or the coast between nine AM and five PM, or after midnight, or during a storm, and on Long Island's north shore one can have Nick Carraway's "consoling proximity of millionaires" without ever having to see them. Perhaps they see us from time to time. But we are always moving, and thus are too much trouble to oppose. Manhattan's hardest working modern tycoons labor as if to maintain open spaces for us, excluding even themselves from spoiling our solitude. Mr. Klann and I must have hundreds of audition cameos on security cameras, yet we have never received a callback. Rarely a living trophy wife is seen to challenge the power of Miss Newmar. She is safe in the forest ponds like a Pre-Raphaelite mermaid. When we cross private driveways in the woods we sometimes encounter delivery trucks. The drivers wave and presume us to be the natives.

We started in the forests at first. After 2012's Hurricane Sandy, hundreds of ancient trees were overturned, and it has become our habit to pause before the umbrellas of their exposed root systems. They seem to suggest opportunities for the arrowhead collector, but we have yet to discover even a single example from a Stone Age hunter. I know that continued diligence will one day yield a find of the pre-Columbian type, but if one broadens the definition of vanished hunters, then it is as if the eye plows the entire field of the woods and exposes countless spear points from a vanished civilization. Take the dilapidations of the Gold Coast's baronial mansion builders for vestigial spear points, and the histories of countless Wall Street big game hunts can be retraced amidst the second growth trees.

Yet these are arrowheads too heavy to carry away, even when they lie in isolated fragments of stone filigree. Nothing important is really vulnerable.

Stand in the woods before the derelict amphitheater or the ruinous swimming pool of Rosemary Farm, and there behold the arrowheads of Roland Ray Conklin, as a "Nimrod the mighty hunter before the Lord." Or observe a hush in the midst of King Zog the First's wreck of a manse in Muttontown, all this amidst a rapidly returning forest and herds of whitetail deer. Conjure the idea of listening to Gershwin's Piano Concerto in the midst of Concord, Massachusetts' Estabrook or Walden Woods, and one has an inkling of the grand conflation suggested by such an arrowhead. Or turn the incongruity on its head, and envision the days when the mansion was new, and at that time asking Charles Ives to play the "Thoreau" movement of his Second Piano Sonata in Zog's ballroom.

Wander on the beach and find arrowhead shards that did not tip shafts but once sat atop great columns, these lying contentedly amidst the vast piles of acorns that come with the richer autumns. No matter the tribe from which one seeks arrowheads, I have found the Thoreauvian concentration about the search to hold true: that one should look for them on high ground, near water, in March—though the industrialist's artifacts are not as dependent on spring rains for their revelation.

Because of the sandy nature of Long Island's soil, a result of its birth by glacier, it is hard for the adventurous runner with eyes trained upon the ground to have much hope of finding traditional fossils. But if one again permits a more liberal hunt, the midnight hour, acting like a freshet to a paleontologist, clears the road and permits one into the center of the street, leaving one undisturbed to study the surface as if it were recently revealed. At the intersection of Main Street and Norwood Avenue in Northport Village, stand over, of a midnight, a fossil trackway of a vanished moment from a less litigious age, when a dog at liberty thought it amusing to leave record of his jog across wet concrete, immortalizing himself like a sauropod. One must wait for the traffic tide to be low to study such things with uninterrupted scholarship.

Yet if one applies their liberal hunt to moments that cannot be preserved by either natural sedimentation or impressions left in man's pavement, behold the rarest of instances on the windy winter beach, when looking back at one's own steps reveals a layer of snow *below* the sand. At the end of that January run of bitter cold and wind, a police officer approached us in his car. He rolled his window down. I expected some sort of reproach. He only observed, having seen us early in the run, far out on the sands that extend into the east edge of Port Jefferson Harbor (quite near where I had noted our remarkable footprints): "You guys are animals!" His words had come to fossilize our fleeting tracks of white.

But the glacier did not fail to leave a collection of immutable things when it created Long Island. The largest of the glacial erratic boulders most often stand singular and separated, either on the shore or in the forest—individual boulders sometimes as large as cars or small structures stationed apart from one another by miles, like foundation stones to the lost glacial mansion, ruins from the Ice Jazz Age. Hence the erratics are as figurative arrowheads, as well. The Dodges, who presided at one time over a large tract of farmland, yet somehow suspecting, perhaps, that they would never leave baronial ruins, long ago carved their family name deep into the side of an enormous erratic on the shore. Thus they chiseled their arrowhead almost after the Indian fashion. But when such boulders are positioned yards away from the beach, and when the tide fails to cover the last inches of their tops, Mr. Klann and I have spent many a pause, sometimes more than once on one shoreline run, fooled by seemingly animate thrashing at and just below the water's surface, only to realize at last it was merely a "rock seal."

Sometimes these erratics stand in groups. I like the collections one finds in the forests. I can never resist standing on them, for then only a succession of mosses or lichens and microns of erosion stands between one's own and a vanished Indian's foot. Mr. Klann and I have also paused before many aging, enclosed, burial grounds, where men have endeavored to leave their own erratics. Some of the headstones are so ancient, that trees emerge directly up from the grave sites. The skeletons in those graves have wooden stakes driven through their hearts from below. They are joust losers from a fight with an acorn.

Just to the northwest of a group of glacial erratics in one forest we came across a tarp hanging over a set of chairs, an impromptu fort built by teenagers. I used to come across such forts in the woods quite often when I was a child. On our present runs we almost never see them; the woods, on this count, seem increasingly pristine in *The Unanswered Question* era. But like glacial erratics in this particular State Park parcel, there are several of these impromptu forts. One had a young person's science book propped into its side wall. Another was constructed entirely of sticks. But usually these teen forts are made from castoff artificial materials mixed with old wood (branches from trees and castoff boards). They are usually surrounded by fire circles and broken bottles—and, in my youth, steel cans. These sites seemed fearsome and dissipated to me when I was child; they still do, in some way. They demonstrate an impulse to start chipping away at the creation of an arrowhead. Better to work away at figurative quartz in the hand than to worship the smooth edges of a phone.

The search for Long Island arrowheads makes one listen, as well. The woods in March are often as mute as a silent film. Mr. Klann has noted in one year's March that not a single bird has sounded during the course of a run in a vast forest only to note the same thing in another year's March in a neighboring woods. Then come May runs, and I note birds in motion all about me, near on the ground, on twigs, and in flight. And it is then that the ears come alive suddenly with recognition. I am sure the sound was there already—as sound is present even when we are sleeping—but I become suddenly figuratively awake to the sounds of the woods. Does one not listen, at times, in the transitional weeks, to the birdsong equivalents to the first buds and shoots? I think not. For a moment after registering the intense visual impression of May birds before me, the woods present themselves as if in a premiere of "The Jazz Singer." The birds sing their complement to the 1920s arrowheads.

One can also be warned by sounds—especially by the crackle of leaf litter—as soon as one takes one step off of a blazed trail at night. Yet one must always be the student, for sometimes even natural certainties are disavowed from the source. For example, a Long Islander always knows that if he travels far enough north, he will hit the Sound; if he travels far enough south he will hit the Ocean. Traveling east, one knows that the Sound is on one's left, the Ocean on the right. Blindfold an observant Long Island native and take him closer and closer to a coastline; he will be able to tell you which body of water he nears by listening. The Sound is without sound. The Ocean makes as much white noise as white foam. But on a day when a distant Atlantic storm is subtly affecting Long Island, an observant native would feel that his inner compass had been sent spinning. A studious native would feel that the poles had reversed. And though Mr. Klann and I moved north one early autumn afternoon and ascended a steep dune in the midst of harbor hill moraine territory, out of sight of water, we heard the Sound's sound. We heard the Sound speak hoarsely. "That can't be traffic," Mr. Klann said after I exclaimed, "What can that be?"

But most formal trail systems have blazes. White blazes are common on Long Island. However, sometimes the snow in winter leaves patches on the sides of trees, all the size of blazes, inviting one to follow bushwhack trails in 360 degrees of horizontal direction, and 180 degrees of vertical. I have seen the snow when it was so new on the side of the trees that it appeared Nature had left blazes pointing in all directions.

Living whitetail deer take the place of the vanished taxidermy of the ruined mansions, and the deer, like the snow, discourage the use of formal blazes. I followed a small herd once along a trail. Then the deer fled off of the path, raising their tails. One in particular caught my eye; one whose hide almost altogether blended with the lovely gray November scene before me. He raised his white tail and seemed to carry a moving trail blaze behind him. Come chase me cross-country, he exclaimed. This example left such an impression on me, that once, even years later, I mistook a clump of new snow, falling from a tree, for a deer's tail, like a diving marker from one of St. Nick's voyages.

Yet *The Unanswered Question* often runs at night. Then one begins to see with one's feet when running on a trail. The process is like sight-reading for a pianist. One cannot look down at their hands when sight-reading. The tree roots which surface on trails may seem like a threat to the timid, but the roots are really like the tactile guidance of the black keys to a pianist. One learns to welcome the roots. The road or the track is as a keyboard made up of only white keys. The woods demand that one play in all keys, more than just C major.

But like a pianist who places too much reliance on his stand light, Mr. Klann and I have given way, at times, to a slackening of self-trust, and when we have lost faith in our eyes at night, it is then that we become the dupes of our efforts at safety. Once, near the edge of the woods, at the northwest corner of a forest opening, we saw what we were sure was some kind of phantom or supernatural appearance. It seemed to move, to hover just above the ground—tall as a man, or taller. It was hard to tell if it was near the ground or near the branch line of the trees. As we approached, it started to appear as an object covered by Christmas lights. I was already chilled by its supernatural appearance, but when it started to suggest an object, small structure, or a figure covered in electric lights, I felt a bit of real fear—fear that it may be the construction of a sort of madman, upon which we were intruding in the dead of night. But when we were close enough we could see that the object was only a group of nearly spent birthday balloons—of that kind made from silvery, thin, shiny, plastic. Our headlamps had provided *all* of the light. Mr. Klann detached the spent balloons from the group and then allowed those that were still airworthy (maybe five or six) to drift up beyond the woods. They cleared the trees and vanished in a northwesterly direction, to land perhaps in the adjacent neighborhood, or perhaps to have a long journey across the Sound before landing again to wish just about anyone who finds them either a very early or very belated happy birthday.

The Unanswered Question Free Running Compact makes its way in its history, at last, to the water, and we have often left the dark woods via power line right-of-ways, and I have remarked that it appeared we were moving up the endless aisle of a cathedral with no altar and no end, and that the high grasses on both sides, shining white in the moonlight, were a congregation.

When we reach the shoreline, I note other lost, silvery, balloons. Every time a piece of driftwood, any kind of detritus of the sea, or a ball comes into our path, Mr. Klann cannot resist casting it into the water. Once we came across a vibrant bright green softball in the sand. I tossed it to Mr. Klann. He thanked me particularly for this example, perhaps because the ball was in such good shape. Out into the water it went. I have asked Mr. Klann why he feels compelled to send into the water all things he finds on the beach. He has given different answers at different times. I suspect he feels something for the shoreline of his native island akin to his regard for the steps of Our Lady of Pompeii on Carmine Street. Mr. Klann would have the steps of Creation as clean as an unscratched vinyl pressing. A week after finding the green softball near Port Jefferson Harbor, we found it again in Mt. Sinai. Perhaps a rock seal had sent it back. But I believe it was because we post the best messages-in-a-bottle to ourselves.

On the shore I sometimes look inland and up to the high sandy cliffs, wooded at their summits. They give often the impression that the island is uninhabited. But once I saw a miniature Niagara of growing daffodils flowing down such a cliff, hinting at the natives that live above the sand and within the trees. Not long ago, when the tide was very high on Asharoken, we were met with a slight challenge from a woman when the tide sent us near to her yard. But if one waits for the moon to change the boundaries, it gerrymanders in favor of the explorer who does not mind sharing the trail with horseshoe crabs, an ancient equestrian trail. At the lowest tides—when the exposed floor of the Sound allows one to run as if on the throat ridges of rorqual whales, as if upon the thumbprint of the

Creator—we have navigated almost the entire edge of our North Shore range (again, from Hempstead Harbor to Mt. Sinai Harbor). At last, it is the shape of these native harbors that has granted the most for me to consider. It is easy to see this range on a map even without consulting the names. On the top of the island it is the series of indentations— pushing water inland in the shape of grand piano lids, in *U-shapes*—that suggests the finger impressions in the handle grip of God.

Every day when I rise I have a view across Northport Harbor—across one of these *U*-shapes, a shape of water thrust into the land by Long Island Sound. Or it is not so much a thrust from without as a vestigial flowing from a vanished glacial river. Via *The Unanswered Question Free Running Compact* I have earned the right to meditate the labor it takes to travel the circuit, the edge of this *U,* to reach the other side on foot—and also most of the *U*-shapes from Hempstead Harbor to Mt. Sinai Harbor, but most intensely those from the Northport Bay area to Oyster Bay. Any attentive scholar's range narrows as his insight broadens.

As a child, I have travelled across by boat from Northport to the Centerport side of Northport

Harbor—by means that are ostensibly direct from shore to shore. But by *The Unanswered Question Free Running Compact* I have worked the edge of the *U*. Only working one's way around the entire *U* of the harbor on foot rewards one with the remembered reversal of their profile though they move in the same direction! Metaphor is only earned by the hardest path. The straight line is *not* direct to metaphorical result. A simple crossing by boat yields little. The straight line to metaphor is the full following of the *U*—and then, after the metaphor is realized, the essence of the interstitial space is removed though its labors are not forgotten.

This *U* effect: It is a metaphor of metaphor formation. This then is *the* crux of *The Unanswered Question Free Running Compact* for me. The *U* effect stands in analogy to all supposed inclemencies— late or early hour; any seemingly prohibitive conditions; lost shoes in the mud—that reveal metaphor leaps and realizations not found by direct routes; that are yet, however, hidden right in our native places.

I sometimes pause during our shore runs and imagine the experiment extended to the greater scale of the Long Island Sound, following its great

U-shape west along the shore until one reaches New York City, then making one's way across the bridges and continuing west along the Connecticut edge as best one can. I would have time, then, to meditate and reconcile my westward-looking profile of Long Island (looking toward Manhattan and my inward and ongoing pull toward an infinite heterodoxy) against my eastward-looking profile on the Connecticut side, the former still in awe of an opposite shore, of a vast an unremitting New England conscience. I am the agent of the green softball's return.

The Unanswered Question adjourns without fail to Dunkin' Donuts after each mission. There we review our notes, and there we partake of large iced teas, which we consecrate as *The Tears of Newmar*.

The Well-Regulated Action: In Defense of the Re-creative Artist

I sometimes meet with apologies from venues when a piano's action may not be serviced to top form. I reply with a smile that such apologies are unnecessary, for in my youth I had to pull up as many keys as push down upon them when playing on battered uprights before elementary school children. In those days I played as often with my palms up as down, like a day at the gym dedicated to both push *and* pull. Once, however, just before a recital in a private South Carolina home, I encountered a woman whose main concern was—though my naked hands were plain before her—that I remove any rings I might be wearing before playing upon her piano's vulnerable ivories.

Something unexplored lurks in the human mind in regard to protecting and maintaining the piano keyboard and its action, and I have been giving this mystery considerable thought. Many people tap their fingers on a tabletop when they are confronted with a dilemma. One might expect a pianist to take double recourse to this outward expression of resolving an inward problem. But in my case—and I have been meditating this puzzle in many places: at my own home piano; while on walks in my native village, during which I study the fossilized trackways of dogs in sidewalk concrete; and, also, at a New York City exhibition opening of paintings by a very noted figure of the piano world—one might note my right foot, at any time during the day, in silent, reflexive action, raising figurative dampers as if onto a still unrealized insight, as if attempting to apply an imagined legato of reconciliation unto considerations too separated to be united by the connective force of equally figurative legato finger action.

We come to pedal all things in our mind; we come to raise the dampers between all events— even the most wildly and seemingly polarized—and endeavor to connect them in the driest halls of our consciousness. Even when the higher part of my mind falls out of this practice, it is not long before a hole forms in the sole of my newest right dress shoe, near the ball of my foot. And even when that hole is just forming, I am made to note it as soon as I walk to a hack accompanist's job in the rain— and my mind goes back to pedaling at all hours.

I have been pedaling hard to connect the three sites I name above, for I have had personal investments in all three, including the last, though I am no painter. But I, too, like many re-creative artists, have felt a compulsion to disavow performance as my main identity. This happened rather early for me, and I turned to writing (novels and essays) over performance art because I was convinced that the former would leave a permanent mark whilst the latter dissolves at once into air. I have discovered that both, however, under the powerful light of honest appraisal, vanish with nearly equal speed.

I met a musician friend, a percussionist, for lunch recently, so that we could discuss the trade of writing. He told me of playing a performance of Haydn's "Creation" with a high level ensemble. A videographer had been employed to document the performance. My friend was proud of his role in the concert. But every time the camera was on him, and he was about to play, the camera then panned or cut away. I told my friend that he should view that panning as Providential, that he should not care to leave his mark as the mere executant of another man's work. Haydn's "Creation" is Haydn's creation after all. I told him that if he has the writer's impulse that following its trade is the way to keep the best intellectual control (true), to say something perhaps utterly new (true), and to leave a lasting mark (false). I say false because when the figurative camera of my mind pans to the spines and folders of my collected written works, it pans then away instinctively before they can speak. We can never watch ourselves.

In the finished basement of my childhood home, stands the piano I principally use still when I practice. Its action is in good working order. In another room of that same basement, for quite some time stood the old Francis Bacon player piano upon which I first learned to play. That piano had very yellowed and ancient authentic ivories, and in many places on its keyboard it had irreparable, stuck, keys. When I would stare at that ruinous action, I often wondered if elephant tusks had been the material of choice because they reminded one that an animal that leaves such mighty footprints has its greatest feature—its tusks—thrashing forever in the unimpressionable air? Was not the suggestive strength of the piano keyboard already in play when mastodons cut the glaciated atmosphere?

But not until recently—though I always knew the tracks were there—did I start to think about how, just below the carpeting underneath both pianos' locations, there is a lengthy fossilized dog trackway in the concrete of the house foundation. One can see the uncovered section of the tracks to this day in the adjacent garage, where they make their way in and out from the driveway. The tracks vanish where the floor of the garage meets the driveway. No one can trace the dog's approach to the foundation from his day of liberty in 1972, and no one can trace where he went after he left by nearly the same path by which he entered.

I have been rising of late from the well-regulated instrument that still sits astride the fossilized dog trackways, and I have been taking walks with my own living dog. He and I have been making a survey of all the fossilized dog trackways in our native village of Northport on Long Island. There are two great examples on Woodbine Avenue, one on Main Street, one on Highland Avenue, one on

Sandy Hollow Road, and a very fine and complex one on Washington Place. Perhaps I started to note the trackways that are available to me that parallel the ancient prints I have visited often at Dinosaur State Park in Rocky Hill, Connecticut. There I have stared down to the trackways and remarked to myself: that if one's work is of value, someday, someone, will note it. For even the casual actions of unmindful dinosaurs from millions of years ago have not, at last, escaped detection.

But as I had felt in my final admonition to my percussionist friend, there seems something false in the permanence of legacies of any kind. I have been taking walks to Washington Place's fossil trackway to think this through. I had discovered recently the Washington Place trackway because I had been compelled to take to its east sidewalk because two little white dogs were out in the yard on the west side of the street. A lady came out to gather them and mutter, to grumble reproaches to her tiny dogs for their combativeness, for I walk with a Rottweiler.

On three squares of concrete right before one house along that east sidewalk of Washington Place, are some splendid fossil prints, leading principally north away from the address, a frozen moment from which the instant before it is hidden, and a moment from which the instant after it is hidden, for the fossils are on only those three squares of an otherwise blank and lengthy sidewalk.

Such fossils always imply humor to me—humor from the printmaker. But the running dog had equal joy on the dry slabs of the sidewalk before and beyond the wet concrete. There is something in the glee that dogs find in locating the wet section, the blank slate, that is roped off to them. Vandals and dogs have no hesitation to christen a new, blank, notebook. They do not hesitate; they do not lose heaps of ideas because they fear what is best to record first—or fear what format the blank journal seems to demand.

The dog pedals with the joyful pant of his living tongue. The concrete tracks are a record of keys that stuck for him. But the solid pavement before and after the tracks were as the better regulated keyboard; they let him race and leave no record. What strikes me is how much a poorly regulated or humidity-plagued piano action stands in analogy to wet concrete on the sidewalk: individual paw prints can be immortalized until perhaps all the blank is taken up. A good action is like a dry sidewalk: always repelling any impressions, always keeping itself clear of print.

A book to its author is somewhat like the wet concrete. It captures the running mind of the writer as it passes over it. The figurative concrete hardens and captures the pawprint traces of his thoughts. But there is an equal amount missing in the record—as much is missing from the book of the run of the writer's mind as is missing from the dog's run over wet concrete when it occurred. There is something very significant about the blank blocks of concrete surrounding the printed areas—the blocks that were there to set the dog to speed and receive him at the end but could take no prints, for they were already dry and solid. At last, the sidewalk sections that record the prints and the adjacent ones that had been dry (and show nothing) seem equal to me. Both sections suggest to me that a re-creative artist's and a creative artist's legacy are ultimately the same. Legacy is, at last, only a well-used present.

The well-regulated keyboard is like that solid, already dry, concrete—and is like the ground leading up to the desk, to the manuscript in progress, to the studio, the easel—as much a trackway itself as it seems but a runway for getting up to speed for the impressionable trackway. In fact, are we not most uncomfortable in the area that takes impressions? Does not the dog shake his paws just after he hits the figurative plaster or manuscript of the concrete? I note that dog fossil trackways rarely double over themselves. And when we part from our own impressionable trackway—the writer's desk, say—do we not seem to take to a fresher, healthier, more sensitive material, dip our pen in a better well, though of invisible ink—the ink like that of the well-regulated action, which keeps no records?

The writer must value that horizontal dash, what lives above the print sections and the unimpressionable slabs, as much as do the performing artist and the dog. The tracks do not immortalize the runner's dash. They only immortalize another witness' review of that dash—or the dasher's review of his own run, in which case he is reduced to another witness, as alienated from his former self as if he is another man. All means of record keeping, all the stuck keys, omit the horizontal, the play of forward and lateral motion. The sticking keys leave a record only of vertical, separate, attacks. The kind of legato I describe is not captured by finger work, pedal work, or even by a recording device. It is only achieved in the mind in the moment. The best reader of any passing moment pedals in his mind and disavows his desiccated tracks. The dog pedals in his horizontal glee, not via his recorded landings. The latter are only as the punch holes in a player piano roll.

Somehow the wet concrete, that which allows supposed immortalization, is no more impressionable than the surrounding hard blocks that accept no prints. The most well-regulated piano action shows no sign of what happened at its keyboard after the playing is over. The well-regulated action shows no sign that one was there after one is gone. It is a like an Etch-A-Sketch toy that shakes and clears itself.

And recordings are like a file, an archive, of stuck keys. Perhaps that is the real reason they become so odious to their creators—and, ultimately, to others—over time? Recordings, even notated compositions, are but signs of stuck keys. They stand in the way of the future. A well-regulated piano is rather like the ground just before and after a track-way; the keys do not stick. The dog who left the fossil prints leaves a clue in his incomplete track-way: that the choice of the wet concrete was not by design, but partial and by chance—part of a greater sequence. Tree roots push the old trackway slabs up, like scores onto the piano's music rack, yet no matter how we play and run, the best mediums (the well-regulated actions, the hard sidewalk), reject all efforts to leave new tracks.

The tangible objects of a body of creative work—the books, the canvases, the scores—are like pianos with irreparable, sticking, keys. Imagine having to cast aside and store each piano on which one has performed after only one use! One would be left with the opposite of a piano showroom; one would be left with a piano charnel house. One would be left with slabs of stored trackways, but soon only a collection of a hoarder's tragedy. The record left on the piano with sticking keys is less important than the record one cannot see in adjacent and perfectly regulated keyboard actions. Who among piano majors has not, late on a weekend night, moved from piano to piano in the vacant practice rooms, as if to rehearse on varying actions? Who has then not thought of such charnel houses but for the work of the piano technician? The piano technician is as a priest in confession—creating the forward moving motion of inalterable blank slates.

These ideas absolve, even vindicate, the concert pianist—or any re-creative or interpretive artist or performer whose medium is time-dependent— from his seeming dependencies on the trackways of predecessors. He lives a sort of hopscotch life in respect to trackways—and would seem to be help-less after the tracks end, and in the area before the start. But whether it is one's own original work or another's, only the living, unrecordable utterance is of ultimate value. I have known many Henrys, but not a one seems to share the same name when I hear it.

Only the most transient creation is the most eternal and ineffaceable. There is no impres-sionable material to record how a solitary con-sciousness improves a moment. A pianist feels his work is written in haste onto atmospheric sheets that are immediately cast into a fire of succeeding silence. But intuition tells me more and more there are no safe and permanent library shelves or secure archives. One comes to suspect that knowledge and achievement are not cumulative, but that growth of mind is really a succession of abandonments.

Always the well-regulated action protects us. We in turn are careful to keep it from proximity to windows and heaters, and we add climate-control devices. We seem to want them so well-regulated that no cavity can ever form on the figurative elephant's teeth; sometimes the strings look like floss meant to tackle tusks.

The well-regulated action works then to push back instantly against all sounded notes, so as to erase the marks of utterance, to keep our philosophy high. The well-regulated action works in analogy to the sun and the moon, working to render blank the shorelines by cleansing tides. Does this not suggest, perhaps, why we favor celestially black lacquer on concert grand pianos? The darkness of the cosmological voids suits the mystery of such instruments.

We are right to worship the achievement of the inventor of the piano's mechanism. One can credit Cristofori for his genius in respect to turning a harpsichord into a piano, but his mechanism's receptivity to later improvement in respect to speed may be its greatest legacy. I notice the common human trait of impatience at elevators—as if repeated pressing of the call button will some-how accelerate an arrival. But on the best pianos the repetition has an answer for every attack. I do not think any facile pianist will disagree that there is no other button that is always so ready to meet our efforts to push it in faster succes-sion. We even have fingerings for this: 4-3-2-1 (or alternate attacks between the two hands on one note). Again, the greatest representatives of mod-ern actions will reset and give a note for each of our strikes. We cannot dance fast enough to leave a fossil on a well-regulated action.

Now that I have lingered over my home piano and one of the fossil trackways in my own village, I wish to tell of the third consideration I named at the start: my recent time at the art gallery on Columbus Avenue in Manhattan. I was early for the 6:00 PM opening, so I spent time alone on one of the benches in the dog park adjacent to the American Museum of Natural History. I watched many dogs run about with glee over a firm, dry, unimpressionable, dust. I entered the gallery after friends arrived, and with all the thoughts I have given above very much in mind, I was struck immediately by the arrangement of the room. On the three interior walls of the small space were the paintings. But of most significance to me was that the gallery was also a performance space. A grand piano stood before the front window; thus it stood principally before a canvas that can hold no images. The canvases that reject permanence—the keyboard and the window—were placed together well.

Again, on the walls perpendicular to the piano were the paintings. If their canvases could have provided the same unremitting challenge as the well-regulated piano and its action before the front window, then those canvases would have been as trampolines to the paint as soon as it had been applied. The paint would have bounced back with each brush stroke; or, like the front window glass, the paint would pass right through and absorb the mark of the artist no more than a footfall on the edge of the tide. But the hanging paintings were as stuck, as sticking keys. The piano stood there as the ultimate, unremitting, blank canvas. The well-regulated action is as an infinitely perfected piece of glass, one that permits no reflections: all of the performer's inner spiritual photons pass through, consigned to an endless outbound journey. The piano keyboard is as a revolving door that leads somehow ever forward. Scratches, fossils from the nails of virtuosos, may remain in the fallboard, but nothing fossilizes in the keyboard below.

What distinguishes the great halls of the different branches of the arts from each other? A library must be expanded, for its shelves begin to creak—even, to a microscopic degree, if its holdings are electronic. The same holds for museums. Their rate of accession must always threaten their space and future. But a performance space does not augment its holdings with time. It deaccessions a work as soon as it is acquired. In virtually the same instant a work is gained, displayed, and then deaccessioned; for it vanishes by a power beyond our will. A concert hall is a library with the most voracious kind of bookworm.

The piano action is as an artist's pencil with tip and eraser on the same end. It resets constantly and always offers no more than the present to its user. Not only does it efface even the record of one's most superior virtuosic predecessors, it erases the record of oneself from even an instant before. I know of nothing that welcomes so much the utterance of only the present moment. Only the player sitting at the bench, sitting perpendicular to the keyboard can hear the performer whose arms move parallel over such a resistant fossil bed.

A well-regulated piano's action will no more let a key stay down than will the water in a pool permit one to keep a ball under the surface. One can keep the ball submerged if complete focus is rendered on that one ball. But let one's focus and downward force be set off balance in any way and the ball pops up—as will the key of any chord if one's proper weight is not maintained upon it, as is often the case with one's outer (and sometimes inner) fingers in wide or densely voiced chords. The well-regulated action will no more retain a shape than a pool of water. But though the glory of public performance may lure many a narcissist to the trade, the action of the instrument at the same time does not permit Narcissus to see himself reflected in the pond of keys.

Probably the only significant fossil permitted to form in proximity to a well-regulated piano action is on the music stand. Perhaps that is the real reason we respect so much those who play from memory. The audience does not so much crave the impression of improvisation as it desires the reassurance of seeing the instrument admit no fossils—seeing the keyboard insist that the canvas is always unfilled, that all prospects are ahead even when time is up. The encores are but preludes.

The grand piano's lid is shaped not unlike an artist's palette. But when the lid is opened, is it not on such an angle that any figurative paint could not but slide away? That surface, too, seems to hint at an unremitting will toward a blank slate, toward an infinite future. Perhaps that is why there is something unnerving to me when I play on pianos in private homes where the lids are closed and covered with family photos and other impedimenta. A pianist craves those things to be removed from the lid. Perhaps many a pianist practices with the lid up because then the symbol of a palette that sloughs away its paint augments the suggestiveness of the well-regulated action that retains no history.

Perhaps the reminder of an unremitting and endlessly demanding future is at times too much for some? Perhaps it is not to keep the dust away that we have fallboards on pianos? When one closes the fallboard of a piano it is like the gesture of closing the eyes of a dead man, for we fear those eyes are still seeing. And, to boot, we often cover a closed piano as if with a shroud. Something lurks within these gestures; they are inspired by more than fear of dust and ghosts.

Under very rare circumstances for a pianist, Nature conspires to augment the perpetual prospective blank of the piano action's canvas. Once, when I had cause to perform on a piano positioned on an outdoor platform, an intense beam of sunlight passed directly over the keyboard for a time. Then it was as if I was challenged by an even greater unimpressionable canvas. The white keys, despite that intense sunlight, were not heated, it seemed, much more than they would have been under other circumstances. C major was not unpleasant. All white keys seem in accord with each other, even though, after close inspection, one will notice that not a one in the compass of an octave is cut the same! I groped the C major sections under that sun as when one walks barefoot in a beach parking lot in summer and strides, tightrope-style, the lightly painted lines of the parking spaces.

But the black keys! The black keys became hot. They were hot enough to make me anticipate the moments when my fingers could leave them. The farther a key signature was from the twelve-o'clock position on the circle of fifths the more uncomfortable it was to touch that keyboard. The sun had augmented the brevity of the action's retention. I cannot recall—even from times under the brightest stage lights—another case when a keyboard presented two temperatures to the hand.

Yet under common circumstances a pianist must warm up his own hands. Most other instruments warm up with the player. But the piano—ever-resetting—for the most part remains cold as the Cosmos, giving harsh but vast reassurance amidst the mortal paintings, amidst the canvas fossils on the walls and the books on the shelves, of a ceaseless breadth of time that is yet to be; as the piano in that Columbus Avenue gallery sat in that center of canvases, silent as a Sphinx, yet not quite radiating riddles nor music yet to be written or played, but, instead, a promise of infinitely incipient and prospective time.

When I left the gallery I walked with brisk steps to the subway, and I kept my eye upon the blank slabs of the cheerful and hard sidewalk, and only looked up to dodge the herds of the professional dog walkers—each living animal with a tongue protruding like a damper pedal from the midst of ivory teeth.

The Conservatory School Address: Coleridgean Reason and the Hack Pianist

This address is in part about the musician who has studied as a concert pianist, but does not pursue the narrow and precise field for which he has been trained, yet does not quit; but does not often play solo recitals nor concerts, nor chamber music, nor strict lieder activities, nor teaches. No, this address will talk about the loner who picks up odd jobs in theater pits, in audition and rehearsal playing—seemingly taking advantage of his higher skills as a reader for performing the labors of a hack. But in these tasks he stays at the piano—free of the terrors of repeating precisely the work of another mind—at ease with music of greater ease, yet making better strides in considering the metaphorical implications of his trade than he could ever do in a classroom, or in practice aimed at a degree recital or a competition or even a concert to be televised before millions; or in the ostensible act of interpreting works that have been held now so long in human hands that they have, to the forward-looking and thinking mind, fallen apart like newsprint amidst wet fingers. Nor does he labor in the conceit that by some untried combination of ancient notes, something new can be composed that does not suggest something old.

Because the expectations for the level of rendering are not often high, and because what is rendered is rarely of an exalted quality, a hack is placed frequently in the best position to observe the metaphorical implications of musical utterance, a position beyond the wildest aspirations of the thinking but, alas, overcommitted virtuoso. The hack logs a count of unthreatened hours of which the virtuoso cannot dream. The hack does not look back on his errors—for he goes into the job knowing he will make them—and he does not prepare, for he does not fear to make the errors. He plays—though often badly—only in the present and never defers his thinking.

Some of my best metaphor hunts have come about from my habit of saying yes to most hack work—even to that for which I should prepare but do not. It takes a real practiced discipline—it takes real preparation—to go into a job unprepared in the traditional sense. But this is quite different from having no shame. I have come to feel most in practice when I have spaghetti fingers. To play well enough to attract notice neither in a good nor a bad way—to leave one free for observation and contemplation at a post suspected to be too busy for observation and contemplation—is the most highly cultivated of seemingly average skills. I rely a great deal on my powers of sight reading, the result of years of discipline—again, allowing me to play well enough to avoid notice, yet protecting me from being forced into specialty.

Though I started earlier, to gain that skill I had practiced unremittingly from age fourteen through thirty. For sixteen years, then, I sat in an almost foetal position—committed to that posture from adolescence to well into manhood. I maintained an umbilical connection to the musical canon before I could judge that canon for myself as an adult. I was not trained enough to judge music before I was trapped in it as a tradesman.

I can now report what I would tell the conservatory aspirant or recent graduate. As a young musician myself I had heard many a lecture on the trial by market that lay ahead for me. But if I were asked to speak to the young in my alma maters, I would put the question to them: Do enough of you subject Music—both new and old, popular and canonical, sacred and profane—not so much to a trial by market in relation to your own efforts as practitioners, but Music to a trial of yourselves, to a trial of you?

Of course I might be held somewhat suspect in all my observations in this address, for I have always worked to master a discipline so that it can at last be dropped and used only for analogy and not for trade. I have never aspired to the stasis of the expert. I have always aimed to toss over my shoulder, plow under, even that discipline of my greatest knowledge, even that of my supposed ultimate vocation—to render it but a point of reference for some unknown future thing. At my recent thirtieth high school reunion I identified my vocation differently to each person who asked what it is I do. The answer was always honest, and somehow the difference was not inspired by the identity of the inquirer.

But I became trapped early in a primary trade

—for I always played just a bit too well for anyone to discourage me from my early and intense pursuit of the piano. Thus I have fallen into music as a profession that I cannot escape; it is my day job.

Once more, I work as a hack. Some of my former teachers, and many who are close to me, object to my use of the word *hack* for myself. Perhaps they are correct, for in using that word I am guilty of engaging in duplicity, guilty in part of false self-deprecation; for my hack work—the depth of field of witness to which I refer—has a very layered meaning for me.

And the supposed pride of pianistic pedagogical descent has never held my interest. I have offended one former professor by leaving teachers' names out of my bio altogether. But would he wish to lay claim to my hack performances? And he cannot lay claim to what I see and witness in my hack renderings. Not even I can claim responsibility for those thoughts. That credit must go to what Samuel Taylor Coleridge characterized as Reason: "Reason is the Power of universal and necessary Convictions, the Source and Substance of Truths above Sense. . . ." I must cite Reason in my bio as my principal teacher.

But if I gave any name in my bio, my first teacher's would be enough. For she showed me Middle C—and that key is as likely to be called B-sharp or D-double-flat. (That any one key on the piano can contain more than one viable and distinct note is due to the musico-grammatical phenomenon known as enharmonics, brought about by the full adoption of Equal Temperament tuning in the eighteenth-century. Equal Temperament divides the octave into twelve equally distanced half-steps, forcing formerly separate notes—like, say, C-natural, B-sharp, and D-double-flat—into a shared space. Enharmonic spellings stand in distant analogy to homonyms in spoken language.) Again, my first teacher showed me enough. For once we are shown Middle C we have been shown how to play the piano; then we spend too much time learning not the piano, but a literature.

That first lesson of Middle C and its enharmonic identities has never failed me, even in the midst of my most ostensibly grim days as a hack. I offer for an example my recent assignment to serve as a sub for Keyboard 2 in the pit of a regional level theater during a summer run. Descending into a theater pit sometimes seems promising to me. The outer edge of the pit—the wall separating the pit from the house—is often slightly curved, that edge suggesting only a small part of an imagined greater circle's arc. Were one to follow the full implications of that circle, it would wrap around much of the outside of the theater's neighborhood. Thus a pit is suggestive of a crater on a partially eclipsed moon. And a completely covered pit is like a fully eclipsed moon: hidden but there, having all the effects of a satellite without being seen at all.

When one descends into a true orchestra pit it feels very much like one is on the surface of a river or pond—of a surface that is, however, below the water. Thus, for the single man, the sunken Pre-Raphaelite maidens are above, on the stage, the hems of their skirts cupped in dance to the deck like upside down flowers over one's head.

But to a trained pianist, the descent into a modern pit is just as often disheartening. The might of a grand piano always suggests to me an athlete in the posture of a one-armed push-up. But to descend into a pit unto a synthesizer is as to climb into a crypt with a deceased beloved and embrace a two-dimensional plastic rendering of her skeleton—as thin and as mass-produced as a page protector, replete with the latter's unwelcome and threatening glare. Even the figurative foot of the deceased beloved, the pedal, slides away with every touch, is attached only by a wire, fastened as if only by a gruesome and exposed tendon. If I were to play—even mildly—with the Lisztian full torso conception of a pianist when sent to the frail bones of the synthesizer, I would be in fear of pushing the keyboard over or of pushing it off of its stand.

The sight of synthesizers is always disturbing. They represent a profoundly negative compression—the kind of negative compression humanity accepts increasingly with virtual reality. The synthesizers in a modern musical theater pit look like patients on tables, patients plugged into wires.

What kind of instrument is it that is as no instrument, that in having so little mass, also has no identity—but is instead a detectable imposter of all its poor multiple false identities? Strange that the principal instrument in such a pit is the one that would go silent, would be the most powerless at the loss of power. I call it the principal instrument for it is the keyboard family that has reigned in respect to our hearing, our sonic culture, since the rise of Equal Temperament. Did not the keyboard command, too, the inevitability of Equal Temperament tuning: the division of the octave into twelve equidistant half steps, presently referred to as 12-TET, permitting one to play in all twelve keys? But when the power goes out now, they (the keyboards as synthesizers) are useless. Even the electric guitar has some communication in a blackout with an acoustic actuality—and of course the electric bass, the reeds, and the drums do, too, in that ensemble into which I descended.

Again, in such a pit, I labored for weeks at Keyboard 2. Yet despite having a speaker (often called a monitor) so that I could hear myself, I could hear myself rarely at all. There were headphones attached to Keyboard 2, but I resisted using them. For some time, instead, I just relished my increasing rage. Surely when a drummer is miked yet plays, too, behind a plexiglass baffle, there is an element of madness in civilization.

For days I played without hearing myself, and for days it was as if I had returned to the time before the eighteenth-century, to the time before Equal Temperament tuning, for the keyboard did not reign on this job. I heard instead an unconscious microtonal supremacy blaring from all instruments and from all the actors above. It was all at a professional level (as far as musical theater is concerned), but without hearing the Equal Temperament reference point coming from myself and my own playing, I lived in the midst of a subtle chaos of the senses—in a chaos without enharmony, a chaos of externally distinct B-sharps, C-naturals, D-double-flats (and every microtone in between). The reed player seated next to me remarked that my description of playing without hearing myself would be like a horn player performing with his bell inserted into a vacuum.

I gave way during one performance and put on the headphones. They placed me suddenly into the Equal Temperament frame of reference: C-natural, B-sharp, and D-double-flat were under one key again, and enharmony placed power within me once more rather than without me. I told the guitarist of this during intermission, and he did not seem to grasp the importance of what had struck me. The headphones threw me back into the grand alloy of Equal Temperament—because I could hear all the subtle lack of intonation in the production once the drums and other noises were pushed away. For me this experience of putting on the headphones was nothing less than a miraculous restoration—a re-entering of the Equal Tempered, the enharmonic world.

So what is it that a pianist detects when under one key one can hear many distinct notes, can feel many distinct notes? What is the miracle of enharmony—that C-natural, B-sharp, and D-double-flat can all reside under one key? I will omit theoretical examples for the same reason that an author of, say, a popular science book on physics will omit equations from his text lest he lose the earnest lay reader with technical proofs that are not required.

And I will not burden this address with attempts to draw too many comparisons between homonyms and enharmonics. When singers in musical theater rehearsals have complained to me that a C-natural and a B-sharp should be written as the same note, I have countered: Would not the costume department have trouble if in a memorandum the following message were written: "To to to tos to many buttons were added" instead of as "To two tutus too many buttons were added"? Again, I will not follow this path further; because homonyms are the result, we imagine, of a sort of convergent evolution in language over time; whereas enharmonics are separate though closely adjacent notes forced into the same locations by an act of human theoretical will, initiated at a self-aware moment in history. But I will say that touching one's fingers to the lips of one speaking homonyms, feeling the slight differences of shape from emphasis and semantic placement—that might be akin to a pianist detecting the change of B-sharp into a C-natural, or C-natural into B-sharp.

I will endeavor to thrive on such analogies.

An enharmonic shift—the moment of its initiation—is as the magic of standing at midnight or during an unplowed snowstorm at the center of a normally busy perpendicular crossroad. Or who has not felt something akin to an enharmonic shift when transferring to a perpendicular track line at a subway stop? An enharmonic shift makes a locomotive roundhouse of a key under the finger of the thinking pianist.

I think the idea of an enharmonic—again, say, C-natural and B-sharp—might be considered from the idea of the pianist hearing—and hearing by feeling with the fingers—one note as level and one as banked or on a slope. A stable tone would feel level; an unstable tone would feel sloped. Yet, again, both are found within the same level key on the instrument. I played in the ballroom of a cruise ship at one time in my life, on a grand piano. While still in port on the first day of the job, I could not understand why I felt suddenly odd and disoriented. But when I took a moment while playing to look across the room and out the window and could see that we were at last moving, then I could comprehend the respelled world—that what had seemed to be my alteration into instability had been really the new instability of the entire room. The room— the entire setting—had changed from stable note to unstable note. A single piano key encompasses a microcosm of this: therein live a mighty ship and its ballroom and its grand piano—all, say, as a stolid and stable C-natural—but therein is also an unstable, watery, B-sharp.

A runner's treadmill can suggest what a shifting enharmonic spelling feels like under a pianist's finger. If I try to rest on it, my fingerings make the note seem as a treadmill belt that will fly me away if I try to remain still, if I try to resist the unstable tone's quality to lead! Imagine, then, that a pianist almost feels a stationary ivory moving from side to side if that key is rendered into an unstable enharmonic identity—feels the key move as if it were a moving treadmill on which one tried to stand still! Imagine that a keyboard is sometimes almost as a treadmill whereon the arms and fingers of the player need no lateral motion, but the keys run as if on their own from side to side—acting like the belt of a moving sidewalk! (The lateral motion of the una corda pedal's action is premonitory of this fanciful idea.) The unstable tone seems stable if one runs at the dictated pace of the musical work at hand; but it will throw one's fingers otherwise, be hot to the touch, if resisted, throw one as when one must take to the sidebars of a fast-moving treadmill if one looks to make an instant stop—when one's legs then are flailed like a too-long tether or chain attached to a rear bumper of a car.

Thus the stable enharmonic counterpart of the unstable note described above may be like running on solid ground. One can leave that note or remain on it by act of one's own will.

When a player feels an enharmonic shift under the finger within one key on the Equal Tempered keyboard, the pianist shifts as from mortal to cyclops. The cyclops is as a symbol of the positive force of our Reason—of our ability, as children of the gods, to perceive depth though we are beings of concentrated and localized perceptions. The cyclops hears enharmony in one Equal Tempered key, hears herds in one atom of ivory. Thus could we have a keyboard with even less keys and hear as much? Perhaps therein is the hint of cyclops conflation! Perhaps the eighty-eight keys could all be one long undivided tusk?

No wonder we sit so long before pianos. The sitting implies the triumph of the Equal Temperament system. Thus, again, indeed the finest piano lesson—the one with most potential information and prophecy—always remains that first one: "Here is middle C; but it is also B-sharp and D-double-flat."

Everything collapses into the premonitory wonder of just one note. Not for nothing does the sound of the solitary church bell, the sole barking dog, the isolated hooting owl, the creak of the lone cricket at autumn's end, the cry of a lone distant locomotive; not for nothing do they work miracles, because they evoke so much within us, and evoke so much within for being so distant—and thus incapable of being hoarded and collected as on a keyboard. Nothing can harm their ability to inspire our greater inner power of division by Reason.

After reestablishing the wonder of a single Equal Tempered note; after, in effect, meditating the significance of my first piano lesson over the course of the pit job I describe above, I took off the headphones and stood up. I left the pit behind and decided to go for a run in the woods before the night was through.

Right at the start of this run, not very many yards into the trail, in a partially open area of the forest, lightning struck so close that for a moment I was forced into a crouch, a crouch as profound as that of a Bill Evans or a Glenn Gould before the piano keyboard. Yet as the day has passed that the great boom of Equal Temperament tuning should inspire us to crouch before the reports of the keyboard, we should not crouch before even the lighting from an actual piano-black sky.

But stand up and face the Cosmos like a tuning hammer, and perceive enharmony even in the seemingly irreconcilable, because it is already there within—demand that compression be realized from the without to the within by each individual will. Even before the lighting we should not crouch like a Gould or an Evans. Nor should we sit or even sit up straight on a piano bench; we should stand before the keyboard of the Cosmos as did my elementary school teachers leading us in the simple songs they learned in Teachers College. We should stand over it all and concentrate Creation from without to within. A positive compression should be worked by every individual ready for the good labor, and a new sort of Middle C will be positively compressed without, yet still recognized as a C-natural or D-double-flat or B-sharp within.

My own skeleton is an ivory, each digit of any finger both a C-natural and a B-sharp. Thus my own self is full of enharmonics. And we walk on the other digits. An organist—from experience with the Equal Temperament pedal board—must feel enharmonics even on the stones of a beach, anywhere he places his feet with more insight than mere locomotion, with more than mere acquisition from the senses. If we really felt the enharmonic glory of the ground of our native places, we would not boast but be ashamed to share our travel photos. Enharmony suggests that a note moves based upon angle of approach—as if Italy or China were to move based upon my point of entry. And would this not obviate my travel if I at last determine the location of my planned destinations? Move rightly and all comes to me.

After graduating from the rudiments of art, from the rich, stationary, and infinitely vast skeleton key to Reason that is hinted at by even one Equally Tempered note and the system of enharmony, later piano works and their latitudinal franticness suggest to me the despair of the modern tourist. The extant literature always seems a defamation, a profanation, of the greater promise in a single note, to what we see and hear within.

What greater invention than Enharmony has there been? What greater invention has there been than one that confirms we need no inventions? It is an invention that proves that our inner powers are always able to survive our external powers to summarize.

I do not know what the new grammars of the new arts and sciences will be, but I am certain that they will come from within, and I will close the piano's fallboard and remain standing as the search begins.

About the Author

Jack Kohl is a pianist and author living in the greater New York City area. He is the author of THE PAUKTAUG TRILOGY: *That Iron String, Loco-Motive,* and *You, Knighted States.*

Made in the USA
Middletown, DE
17 March 2019